WEIRD SANTA

& other Xmas Tales

Brian Allan Skinner

Nighthawk Press

TAOS, NEW MEXICO

Nighthawk Press
PO Box 1222
Taos, New Mexico 87571
www.nighthawkpress.com

Book Layout & Design by Brian Allan Skinner
Cover art: "The Heart of Christmas" © 2019 by Brian Allan Skinner
www.brianskinner.net

Publisher's Note: This is a work of fiction. Names, characters, places, and incidents are a product of the author's imagination. Locales and public names are sometimes used for atmospheric purposes. Any resemblance to actual people, living or dead, or to businesses, companies, events, institutions, or locales is completely coincidental

Weird Santa / Brian Allan Skinner – 1st edition
ISBN 978-1-7334483-1-4
Library of Congress Control Number: 2019952261

CONTENTS

ACKNOWLEDGMENTS

"The Christmas Village" first appeared, in substantially the same form, in the anthology *Christmas Blues: Behind the Holiday Mask*, published in 1995 by Amador Publishers of Albuquerque, New Mexico. Little did I suspect that I would one day be a *Nuevo Mexicano* myself. But that's the way life's arabesques twist and turn and bring us to where we should be.

"Weird Santa" first appeared in my collection of short stories called *Shoot Me, Jesus: Tales of the Old & New Southwest*, published by Nighthawk Press in Taos, New Mexico, 2018.

"Never Too Old, Never Too Late," is from my previous collection of fiction, *The Magic of Kindness: A Novel in Short Stories*, also published by Nighthawk Press in 2019.

I wish to thank Mary Skinner and Anthony Fountain for encouraging me to complete this collection of short fiction—not least of all by their reading earlier drafts and offering suggestions. Dianne Vona and Sandra Richardson helped me improve these tales immensely, offering their ideas and advice in our weekly workshops, "Peerless Critique," held at the Society of the Muse of the Southwest.

Special thanks are owed to Joseph Montagna for planting the idea of an anthology of Christmas stories, all by a single author. I did not promise anything to my friend when he proposed it. My muse does not always cooperate with my own ideas, much less someone else's. Even recalling the publication of my previous Christmas tale, two stories hardly comprised a book. Was Joe serious?

Once the seed had been planted, however, I found Joe's suggestion irresistible. My muse inclined to agreement and ideas came from every direction, despite the fact that I was simultane-ously at work upon *The Magic of Kindness*, my second "novel in short stories."

My creative writing student, Otto Manley, gave me the prompt during one of our writing sessions for what became "A Doggie's Tale." I repaid him by naming the mutt in the story "Otto."

I wish to assure you that *Weird Santa: & other Xmas Tales* brought me immense pleasure. I hope the stories brighten your Christmas, too, no matter which of the three-hundred sixty-five days of Christmas it happens to be.

Brian Allan Skinner

AUTHOR'S NOTE

There are at least a few things from my childhood I have not quite outgrown. Christmas is one of them. As I hope you will be able to tell by reading the ten stand-alone tales in the present anthology, I am very fond of the Christmas season.

Borrowing from both Charles Dickens and O. Henry, and the original Nativity story of course, I believe that Christmas is a time of redemption and conversion. The hard edges of hard hearts are softened. That notion lies at the core of each of these short stories.

I have had more than six decades of Christmases upon which to draw for inspiration, going all the way back to my fourth Christmas, the first I still remember.

My mother decided, using an aerosol can of artificial snow, to flock our fresh balsam fir. She did this, however, after my dad had strung the lights on the branches. When the bulbs heated up, they started smoking. My parents debated calling the Chicago Fire Department, but the danger had passed once the snow "dried up." The fake snow speckled the Christmas lights with brown spots. Each year, as a few of them burned out, they were replaced with new bulbs that did not have "freckles."

Once again I hope you enjoy this collection of tales. Please take a moment to share your comments with me and other readers, either on my Amazon author's page or through my web-site at www.brianskinner.net. I look forward to hearing from you.

Merry Christmas.

Brian Allan Skinner

THE CHRISTMAS VILLAGE

Delia sits at the kitchen table and stares at the cold sludge at the bottom of her coffee cup. It doesn't seem like Christmas to her. She tries to remember the last time she was in a holiday mood—about ten years ago.

Jim pushes open the kitchen door with his foot, his arms laden with fluffy rolls of cotton batting. His hair is dusted with snow. He smiles. There is a bounce in his walk. He squeezes through the doorway to the living room, whistling "Joy to the World" so off-key it is unrecognizable—except to Delia, who has been listening to it for a month.

She pushes herself away from the table and pours another cup of coffee. She slumps into the chair in her pink fuzzy bathrobe and warms her hands on the steaming mug. Delia wishes she could go back in time and nip Jim's obsession with Christmas in the bud. With the clarity of hindsight, she knows exactly how it started. And it was entirely her fault.

The twinkling lights from the living room swim in the dark liquid abyss of her mug. She stirs the coffee into a whirlpool that sucks down each of the colorful reflections, pulling her down into a melancholic recollection of a Christmas past.

⎯⎯⎯⎯⎯◦⎯⎯⎯⎯⎯

Ten years ago, Jim did not even shop for his own undershorts. Delia suspected something was afoot when he agreed to accompany her to Wally's Discount World the week before Christmas. Jim pointed out each tinsel-draped display of marked-down Christmas items, every glittering gewgaw and cheap stocking-stuffer, as though he were visiting from a small village in Eastern Europe. They lingered particularly long in the aisles crammed to the ceiling lights with Christmas decorations, even though their attic held enough lights and ornaments to festoon a forty-foot Douglas fir without cheating a single branch or needle of its cheerful burden.

Jim stopped as if a wad of chewing gum anchored him to the floor.

"Look at those," he called to Delia. "And they're on sale, too."

He stood in front of the shelves laden with cheap little made-in-China cardboard houses, the kind that one would arrange into a circular village beneath the Christmas tree on a fluffy skirt of cotton batting to represent snow. One bulb from a string of lights would be stuck into the round hole at the back of each house to show that miniature families lived in them.

Delia thought the toy houses looked especially cheap that year. The glistening mica snow had been sprayed at angles from which no storm could approach unless it had descended out of a whirlwind, depositing a blanket of snow even on the underside of the eaves. The spongy lichen trees had been glued to the bases in postures leaning into the make-believe blizzard rather than away from its blasts. The cellophane windows had been stuck on so haphazardly they could have been designed for miniature fun-houses. The church steeple slouched at a precarious angle, and the small shops were marked with crooked signs announcing "Candies Shoppe" and "Toys Shoppe."

"You can't be serious, Jim," Delia said, moving aside to let the bottle-neck of shoppers pass around them. "They're ugly, and cheap-looking, and they're probably a fire hazard. See? They don't have any UL stickers on them."

Jim seemed disappointed by her remark. "But the price is certainly right: $9.99 for the whole village. Come on, Delia. I never say a word about how you spend our money. Are you telling me I can't get one lousy little Christmas village for ten bucks?"

"It's not the money, Jim. It's how cheaply-made and tacky they are. What on earth would you want them for?"

"Because I had a Christmas village as a kid. I like the stupid thing, OK? Do I have to sign a voucher or something?"

Delia relented, deciding that $9.99 was not worth an argument one week before Christmas. That was her first mistake. She told herself at least it will be under the tree. She had enough long, spiraling icicles and spread-winged angels to conceal a model of Manhattan beneath the lowest branches.

Jim's impatience with the rest of their shopping caused Delia to suspect that her husband had got what he set out to find once the "Olde Tyme Xmas Village" had been loaded into their cart. She also suspected that, back at home, she would find a wrinkled, dog-eared page in the Sunday advertising supplement with just such an item in it. The photograph in the ad would show the first models to roll down the assembly line rather than the tired little houses churned out by the weary Chinese factory workers trying to make a few extra yen in overtime before Christmas.

She wondered what the Chinese workers thought of the odd little trinkets they made, such as Pez dispensers and Groucho Marx glasses. After making all these Christmas villages would they think that every American house had a huge round hole in its windowless back side? What would they imagine the hole was for?

That year's family Christmas presents—mostly electronic gadgets in large boxes packed with molded Styrofoam—did not allow enough room under the tree for Jim's village, so the shops and houses were set up in a Main Street straight line on the mantel. Jim removed the clock, the brass candlesticks and Delia's paperweight collection, setting the village up on fresh rolls of Red Cross cotton.

Delia considered Jim's arrangement suitably festive, so she raised no strong objections. She did not care for the effect created by the portraits of Jim's grandparents hung above the mantel, the old couple staring down sternly like disapproving deities plotting an assortment of natural disasters about to befall Jim's cheerful village. She let all of that pass. She doubted the Christmas village would survive the next summer in their hot attic. What didn't fuse together in the August heat would probably come unglued. She needed only to worry that the discount stores would again carry the cheap cardboard shops and houses. Maybe she could write a letter of complaint to Underwriters' Laboratories informing them of the potential hazard.

———————◦———————

The holidays over, Delia looked forward to having an uncluttered mantel for the next eleven months. Jim did not give her that long, however, to take a vacation from the thought of his village. That June, on their holiday trip through the Ozarks, Jim stopped at every gift shop and tourist shack selling handicrafts. Unfortunately, he hit it lucky at the first such shop, a ramshackle addition to the gas station, where he found a pair of popsicle-stick log cabins with papier-mâché fir trees. The miniature cabins had been intended as holders for salt and pepper shakers. Jim planned to drill holes in the backs of the log cabins large enough for a seven-watt Christmas tree bulb. He asked Delia if she had any use for a couple of extra salt and pepper shakers.

She did not say the first thing that came to her. "Why not make snowmen out of them?" she said instead.

Jim heard none of the sarcasm in her suggestion. "Great idea!" he said, and was then on the lookout for a drugstore to buy more rolls of cotton. Delia and the kids stayed in the car, sipping their warm milkshakes.

In late June it had not been so difficult to put aside thoughts of snow on the roof and Jim's village coming down from the attic. But by the end of October, around the time the first stores began putting up their Christmas displays, Delia could not avoid the subject. Jim brought out the boxes he had stored in the hall closet and began unpacking his summer's worth of acquisitions in miniature real estate. He even drew up a blueprint for the layout of his village.

It became clear to Delia that the boom-town Christmas village would no longer fit on the mantel. Jim set to work out in the garage, building plywood extensions to the mantel. She said nothing, having learned her lesson with her fanciful suggestion to turn salt shakers into snowmen. Her sewing basket had been ravaged and now the button-eyed miniature snowmen stared at her from across the room.

––––––––––⬤––––––––––

Each holiday season the village grew, as though speculative hordes of land developers had descended upon the bucolic tranquility of the tiny town. Jim spent their vacation trips and three-day weekends scouting garage sales, flea markets, and church bazaars in search of more items for his village. The miniature houses were no longer his main concern. He had dozens still to be unpacked and worked into the snowy setting. Jim now needed all the things that went with village life: the streetlamps, mailboxes, doghouses, cars, pedestrians, skaters, sledders, carolers, and snowmen.

Delia had been dropping hints to their relatives and friends not to buy any more miniature items for Jim. The village had expanded to cover all three windowless walls in their living room, reaching upwards on additional shelves nearly to the ceiling, and downwards two more shelves practically to the floor.

But Delia's requests were ignored. It was easy for people to shop for Jim. They didn't have to think about what to get him and he liked whatever he got. He could always use a few more streetlamps, especially the battery-operated kind that did not need to be wired up.

Jim and Delia tended to get more company during recent Christmases than they had been used to. Jim's village became an attraction, while Delia's Christmas tree—as meticulously decorated as ever—was all but ignored. Jim's village became the reason people visited. They never got further than the living room, content to gaze at it for hours on end, delighting in finding scenes they hadn't noticed on earlier passes.

Their enjoyment puzzled Delia. The village was cute and clever only from a distance. All the magic disappeared for her upon closer inspection. Nothing matched the style of anything else. The scale of things was way off. There were streetlamps from an old train set that towered above the church steeple. There were sledders so huge they could only have fit into the houses through the large round holes on their back sides. The skaters had come from so many flea markets that they were of such unmatched sizes and periods of dress they seemed like a freakish carnival skating across the glitter-dusted mirror. There were toy cars unable to fit in any garage and pedestrians tall enough to look face to face with second-storey occupants gazing out their crooked cellophane windows. To Delia, it was as though Charles Dickens and Rod Serling had collaborated on a theme park.

Doesn't anyone notice all these discrepancies? Delia wondered. *Were they simply dazzled by all the blinking lights?* Try as she would, she could not manage to see the charm of her husband's Olde Tyme Xmas Village.

There was now less and less of each year that Delia did not have to look at this surreal assemblage of cardboard, plastic, wood, and ceramic pretending to be a normal village. Last year it had taken him until the middle of April to put everything away and allow Delia to reclaim the living room.

This year, Jim had told her he planned to get a head start on setting up his village over the extended Labor Day weekend. Out came the boxes and rolls of cotton, the plywood shelves, and the stapling gun.

Delia had wanted a quiet barbecue in their back yard with just a few friends over. She could hardly get Jim to take ten minutes away from his project.

"Jim, please come out here and mingle, will you?" she called.

"In a minute, dear. Just let me finish up this one string of lights."

"All right, but then that's it. This is a holiday."

Jim eventually came out to the patio. It had been a long string of lights. The hamburgers and chunks of Italian sausage were indistinguishable from the unlit charcoal briquettes at the edge of the barbecue kettle.

No tactic Delia could devise ever got Jim to give up or delay his project. She did vow to herself, however, that it'd be over her dead body that the Christmas village would be allowed to sprawl beyond the living room. It was the only time she'd put her foot down.

By Halloween, Jim had the shelves installed in the living room and began setting out the first houses according to his numbered and color-coded master plan. He relinquished part of one evening to carve a jack o'lantern, and then went back to rolling out the cotton. On Thanksgiving, Delia had to enlist her sister's husband to carve the turkey. Jim had become entangled in the public works project that would bring light to Main Street.

The Youngs' two children, Janet and Ricky, rarely brought their friends over once their father had started setting his village up in the living room. It was not so much his peculiar obsession that embarrassed them. Rather, their friends became so engrossed in looking at all the miniature scenes and in watching their father set up a new neighborhood that they hardly paid attention to Janet and Ricky.

Ricky now let his girlfriend wait for him on the front porch, ever since she had got so caught up making suggestions about how to place a row of houses on a terraced hill of cotton that she and Ricky missed the movie they had been looking forward to for weeks. Ricky wished for a father with more normal pastimes: one who watched every football game broadcast and who simply grunted in response to all remarks and questions.

"Hand me that hardware store over there, will you, Ricky?"

"Pop, where's it all going? I mean, don't you ever stop? It's like you're still playing with toys. Here."

"Thanks. It needs a new bulb. The box is under that roll of cotton. I guess I never thought of it that way: *playing with toys.* Maybe you're right," he said, chuckling.

With that single remark of his father's, all the air was let out of Ricky's argument. You just couldn't insult him enough to get him to give up his Christmas village. The whole family had tried.

This year, Jim added a new feature to enable the children and shorter adults to see how those on the upper tier of shelves lived. He built a wooden platform with three steps. To the handrail at the front of the platform, he attached a small telescope. Delia and Janet and Ricky knew at once from where Jim had drawn his inspiration: from all the scenic overlooks with stubby, coin-operated telescopes at which they'd spent a few moments during their vacation trips to gift shops.

The living room furniture was clustered in the center of the room, sofa and chairs back to back, with the viewing platform at one end of the group. As a touch of authenticity, Jim placed a hand-lettered sign, "Please Watch Your Step", on each of the three risers to the viewing platform. Janet's calligraphy set had been nearly depleted of inks before her father got the lettering just right. He had chosen Old English script, in keeping with the holiday theme.

The whack! whack! of Jim's staple gun awakes Delia from her depressing reverie, driving the thought of Christmas into her. Whack! It is nearly ten o'clock in the morning and she's still sitting in her bathrobe. She intends to keep the few remaining Christmas customs that Jim has not ruined for her, and hopes she has enough energy and enthusiasm left to make at least one batch of rumballs.

The steady tramping of visitors up the walkway has not been impeded by the heavy accumulation of wet snow. If anything, it seems to add to their enjoyment of the season and their appreciation of Jim's village, which they can view in all its snow-blanketed charm without having to shovel any of it. With the fireplace roaring, it is warm and comfy in their living room.

Delia grows tired of answering the front door. She is getting nowhere with her Christmas baking. She scrawls a note and tapes it to the door, asking visitors to let themselves in. She sets out two boot trays and unrolls plastic runners from the entrance hall to the observing platform. If they had charged only a quarter per head, Delia figures, they could have paid off their mortgage. But Jim objected to the idea, saying it didn't coincide with his notion of the spirit of Christmas.

What is Christmas about? Delia wonders. She had once looked forward to the holidays and enjoyed every minute of their brief stay. Jim's stupid village has ruined all of that for her. She now dreads the holidays and overlooks any reminder of their coming as handily as she tucks away and tries to lose her dental check-up reminders. Why can't she get into the spirit of Jim's innocent pastime? Everyone else seems to enjoy it, even the strangers steadily trudging up their walkway. What is she missing? What's wrong with her?

Every Christmas tale requires its King Herod or its Ebenezer Scrooge, just for contrast. Delia has somehow been cast in the role without ever trying out for the part. She vows to change that. After all, conversions are an integral part of Christmas lore, too. She takes her last tray of cookies out of the oven and makes herself a pot of tea, which she laces liberally with some the liquor remaining from the batch of rum-balls. A healthy dose of rum spills into the teapot.

Delia settles on the sofa next to Jim, allowing the glimmer and glint of miniature streetlamps to sparkle in her blurry vision. The Christmas warmth spreads through her like a viscous fog. She is a little drunk and begins to feel sorry. She takes hold of Jim's hand and squeezes it. Not feeling up to words or apologies at the moment, she leans against his shoulder and hums, getting sleepier and cozier with each sip of tea.

The periphery of her vision suffers a rum-induced collapse. Delia can no longer focus on the room or the furniture. She sees only the village, sparkling with tiny lights and mica-crusted snow. It's like being outside in mid-winter without the inconvenience of a bulky coat and sound-damping hats and scarves. The blasts of pelting snow cannot touch her.

The doorbell rings in the middle of her reverie. Jim pulls himself up from the sofa and opens the front door. A six-year-old boy has come to see the miniature village. His snowsuit looks as though it has been pumped full of air. He waddles along the path of plastic runners, the snow slipping from his head and shoulders in muffled thumps.

Jim helps the boy out of his hooded snowsuit. An oval of

bright red skin lights up the center of his face.

"My mom says I can only stay till six o'clock. We're going to open all our presents after supper," the boy announces

"We'll let you know when it's time," Jim assures him. He takes hold of the boy's hand and helps him climb up to the viewing platform. "Watch your step," he adds.

Delia feels as though she has been swallowed up in a snow bank: a deep, warm, sleepy pile of snow. She extracts herself from between the sofa cushion and gets up. She brings a plate of her cookies and a glass of milk to the boy. He hesitates, as though he doesn't know whether to admire the cookies or eat them. He takes a bite of a sugar-sprinkled butter cookie and puts his eye up to the toy telescope.

"Neat," he says, swinging the telescope around and nearly toppling from the platform.

"Why not come down for a minute?" Jim admonishes. "You'll be able to see the streets on the bottom much better. Just don't touch anything."

"I won't," he says.

The boy walks around the room, leisurely viewing one tier at a time. Delia follows him with the plate of cookies and a cordless vacuum.

"What's your name, son?" Delia asks.

"Tony."

"Well, it's almost time to go, Tony. You wanted us to remind you."

"Oh," he says. "I don't really have to go home. Mommy and Daddy were fighting again, so I always go outside to play when they fight. I just came over here 'cuz I got cold. I saw the Christmas town last week. Can I stay a little bit longer?"

"We'll have to ask your parents," Delia says.

"OK," Tony replies, and recites his phone number to her as if it were a commercial jingle.

Delia goes into the kitchen. Her tongue has grown a little thick. She can hardly think how to phrase what she wants to say to the boy's mother.

The woman on the other end of the line sounds distraught.

Her voice is all in her nose, as though she had a terrible cold, or has been crying.

"He talked about that toy village of yours all week," the woman says. "We're not quite ready for Christmas yet. But I don't want him getting in your way. Just send him home when he gets to be a bother."

"But it's dark out," Delia reminds her.

"He knows the way home. Just tell him when you've had enough of him. Thanks for your trouble. And Merry Christmas."

"Merry Christmas," Delia echoes. She holds the buzzing receiver. She isn't quite sure what's been decided on. She gets herself a cup of black coffee and sets the dining room table for their Christmas Eve supper, setting an extra place.

When Janet and Ricky return from last-minute shopping with their friends, they say nothing about the extra plate and the little boy who announces to them, "That's where I'm gonna sit." When their father sets Tony on his shoulders, straddling his ears, and takes him on a close-up tour of the upper terraces of the village, Janet asks her mother what's going on.

"Your father keeps busy with his hobby," Delia says. "Here, bring the casserole along, will you? Maybe I have too much time on my hands. Maybe I need a hobby, too."

"What, taking in orphans?" Janet asks.

"You gotta be kidding," Ricky says.

"Well, why not? You two are pretty much on your own. I've got the time. I could call the Volunteer Center. There are plenty of kids out there who need a little extra attention. I could always become a Den Mother or something. Please go call your father and Tony in to supper. The food's getting cold."

Throughout the meal, Janet and Ricky remain silent. No one has to worry about keeping a conversation going. Tony does enough talking for everybody.

After supper, Tony grabs hold of Janet with one hand and Ricky with the other, and leads them into the living room. He takes them on a guided tour of The Olde Tyme Xmas Village as though they might not have noticed it before.

"I don't get it," Ricky tells his sister. "Are we from another planet or something? I really don't get it."

"Me neither," Janet says, lurching forward as Tony tugs on her arm.

The boy keeps them in tow, dragging them along with the enthusiasm of a real estate agent who suspects the young couple might have inherited some money.

Delia settles back in the sofa cushions next to her husband. It is still early on Christmas Eve—plenty of time, she thinks, for a couple of more conversions. The miniature lights sparkle in her eyes.

The Olde Tyme Xmas Village glows with renewed effort, too, as though conjuring up one last trick on behalf of the hard-hearted.

WEIRD SANTA

My parents were an odd pair. My mother was a former Catholic nun, though not yet former at the time of my conception. My father owned a pizza joint near Columbia University at the time my mother worked on finishing her doctorate in astrophysics, compliments of the Benedictines. They fell deeply in love despite struggling against it. They enjoyed their honeymoon here in dusty old Red Willow, New Mexico, and never went back to New York.

What they had in common eluded everyone save an oddball friend they shared. His name was *Nicolás*, pronounced in the Spanish way. I have not witnessed a happier union than my parents' in my three decades on the planet. Their love was an elemental force and its warming rays enfolded me as well.

I'm proud to have my mother's intelligence and my father's calm control. My father, even when it was clear he was right, would say, "Oh, they'll discover their mistake." He was far from weak, but his patience exasperated my mother and me. My mother on the other hand, at the slightest slight, fired off incomprehensible volleys at full volume until she sounded as though she'd gone mad. My position between them meant that I tolerated an awful lot of crap, but when my lid blew, the explosion could be heard for miles.

My appearance melded my mother's flaxen-haired Nordic beauty and my father's curly-haired Mediterranean swarthiness. On most days I felt attractive, but on others I considered myself a girl designed by committee.

On my fourteenth birthday, my mother and father, Hildegard and Oscar, told me what a "stellar" young woman I was "evolving" into. Those were their words.

"You seem as capable of taking care of yourself as I was at that age," my mother told me, failing to mention at my age she resided in the cushy digs of the Benedictine Order House in Binghamton, New York. "The time has come for your father and I to fulfill our own destinies. I'm afraid we must leave you."

"Leave? For how long?" I asked.

My father turned and looked at her.

"Probably forever, my dear, sweet child. We're going up The Mountain."

"What're you saying?" I realized I sounded whiny.

"We will be following our shaman to the top of The Mountain to learn how to bring the world into existence each morning. It takes many years of study. We must stay on when the old holy man dies."

I knew by my father's tone that their minds were made up. I suppressed a grin. *C'mon. Really? A shaman?* I thought, and started to cry.

"You'll be very well provided for," my father said, unable to look me quite in the eye.

"Mom. Dad. Are you serious? I'm fourteen years old. Not yet. Please," I begged.

"Well, then, when, Hypatia?" my mother asked. "Many children lose their parents at a much younger age. We want you to have plenty of time to become who you are, dear, without our getting in your way."

"Gee, thanks. How 'bout three more years?" I asked, trying not to sound too pathetic.

They glanced at each other and then at me. They nodded.

"You have us for another three years, child," my father said, giving me a gentle hug and a kiss slightly salty with tears.

My mother hugged us both. Ever the practical one of the pair, she advised me, "And please don't waste us on silly teenage tantrums, dear. Grow out of them before we go away. You can have them later in life if you like. Many of our friends do. Red Willow's just the place."

It was some of the best advice I ever received. They were the three happiest years of my life, too—at least so far. And, contrary to what I expected, I miss my parents more as time goes by, not less.

———————⋗◦⋖———————

On my seventeenth birthday, at our little family party before my friends arrived, my father handed me a thick investment portfolio carefully wrapped in sappy birthday paper.

"You will never have to worry, dear child."

"I don't anyway, Daddy. It doesn't change anything. A total waste of time."

"God bless you, Hypatia, wise beyond your years," my mother remarked.

My mother handed me her own small package. It contained the deed to their house and the keys to her eighteen-inch Newtonian telescope, to the motorized drives that moved the beast. She lost her composure and ran to my father, burying her face in his shoulder and sobbing.

I nearly broke down myself when I was saved by the doorbell. It was my friend Ginnie from school. She held a shiny foil package tied with sparkling red ribbon—entirely her style. My parents introduced themselves and then disappeared into the kitchen.

When the bell rang again, it was their strange friend, the skinny old guy the rest of town called "Weird Santa." Now I knew who their "shaman" was. I pointed Nicolás—if that was his name—towards the kitchen. I heard them exchange blessings, and then the back door closed. I told my friend Ginnie my parents were running away from home.

"Oh, my God," she screeched. "What're you going to do?"

"Uh, let me see. My parents will be out of the house, not coming back. I have the keys to the liquor cabinet. My friends are coming over. What d'you think I'm going to do?"

"Aren't you sorry?" Ginnie asked.

"Of course I am," I told her. "But that won't bring them back. I'm trying to make the most of my changed life. What d'you expect? I'm a teenager."

The doorbell rang. It was Helen and Alice and Alice's ugly, big-eared boyfriend. Word must have spread. Someone invited a Turkish techno band called Brief Heavy Downpours who played loud enough to crack two windows. There was no one the neighbors could complain to any longer. I was now the majordoma. Too bad.

Somebody brought pizza, but it wasn't from my Dad's place. It was pretty bad. I had a long make-out with a boy I didn't like and sampled more flavors of alcohol than I knew existed, including one with a worm in the bottle which the boy I didn't like coaxed me into swallowing. It must have been the worm. I spent the night and next morning in the bathroom.

When I awoke at the crack of noon, I was alone in the big old hacienda. I thought of my parents and cried for three hours—on and off, but mostly on—until I was as dry as the desert wind blowing into Red Willow. I haven't touched alcohol since. Or worms.

I never laid eyes on my mother and father again.

I remained convinced the odd fellow who followed my parents from New York and hung around the house every year at Christmas was the same guy everyone in town called "Weird Santa." I know he had something to do with getting the behemoth Newtonian telescope from upstate New York out here to New Mexico from my mother's Order House.

Nearly all the citizens of Red Willow had an encounter with Weird Santa at least once in their lives. It was certain his mottled gray-and-white beard was genuine, yet no one in town sported such chin whiskers. Where did he hide out the rest of the time? Many of us had received one of his insanely appropriate Christmas gifts, meticulously wrapped geometric solids that bore no relation to the shape of the object inside. He knew each of us by name and remembered enough of our situations to qualify as more than a casual acquaintance. The *Red Willow Reporter* offered a one-thousand-dollar prize to the person who could unequivocally identify him. It has gone unclaimed for the past five years.

Last December, a dozen years after my parents went away, I stayed with my friend Ginnie in Santa Fe the week before Christmas. She had a boutique of hand-made punk turquoise jewelry, all of it too big and painfully ugly. It was wildly popular, and she was considering opening a second shop in Red Willow. Weird Santa accosted me in the parking lot and added another bundle to my overladen arms.

"Your mother and father are very well, Hypatia. They are quite adept at calling up the moon and it is only a matter of time before they can call up the sun by themselves. Stay warm, child."

Before I could peek around the packages he was gone, up the street handing out a box in silver foil to another bewildered shopper. I dropped his present fumbling with my car keys. It did not appear to be broken: nothing tinkled or rattled. I set my purchases in the back of the car and unwrapped it. One box nested inside another like Russian dolls. The gift was a log, not even a whole log, but a split log. *Just what I need*, I thought, and put it back among the other packages.

It began to snow around Española and did not let up for the rest of the drive home. The temperature had plummeted, too. I was eager to get warm and snug.

A yellow sticker hung from the front doorknob. It did not look like good news. I fetched the presents and the half-log from Weird Santa and rushed inside.

The house was freezing, probably just a degree or two above the pipes bursting. The notice on the door had been a disconnect order from the gas company. Just great. And no one available for the next three days to reconnect my service—and my heat.

It was exactly like my latest ex, Elliot, to maintain his nano music service but forget to pay the gas bill. He'd left two weeks before, saving me the trouble of kicking his ass out at Christmas. His crap was already rotting in the *Eco-Happy Landfill*. I felt much more agreeable since he left, the best Christmas present he could have given me. But it was good-bye to boyfriend number five, the fifth in five years, each one's name beginning with the letter "E," the fifth letter. I wondered, *Was there some kind of message here or was every datable man in Red Willow a loser with the intellectual life of a mushroom?*

I put the log from Weird Santa in the fireplace in the living room and lit it with the paper and cardboard from its wrappings. It caught quickly and put out a good deal of heat for its size. I stretched out my fingers. I would be warm for ten minutes. What then? And I'd have to drain the water system before the pipes froze. Merry Fucking Christmas.

That dear little Yule log continued to pump out heat and a cheering glow for three more hours. I gave up before the fire did and went to bed. Even my bedroom, furthest from the living room, was toasty. I was beyond figuring it out just then. Weird Santa's gift was insanely appropriate. He'd known exactly what I needed this year. Merry Christmas.

———————⊃●⊂———————

It is Christmas Eve again, a year later, my second holiday season without a boyfriend. If Weird Santa wants to bring me something I can really use, it'd be a man. I'm not ready to settle yet for just any man, though maybe I might in another week.

I regret there is still no boyfriend Number Six, but maybe that's for the best. I had many wonderful Christmases with my parents. It's the one time of year I associate particularly with them and their weird friend. I miss them, and I don't need another know-it-all boyfriend spoiling Christmas for me and getting me upset.

The log from Weird Santa is still burning twelve months later. It must be impregnated with some nasty petrochemicals, but it beats hauling firewood, cleaning out ashes, and choking on smoke. I don't know what's going on, but I'm sure it's not magical. My parents, I'm afraid, believed in such nonsense, and unusual abilities some called "paranormal" were ascribed to them. I lived with them for seventeen years and never witnessed anything that wasn't normal parental weirdness. Well, except maybe once.

I wanted to know if my parents were still doing it, you

know, making love. I waited until I heard their bedroom door close, and sneaked around to the back of the house and peeked through the window. They had candles burning everywhere. It was miraculous they didn't burn the house down. My parents floated several feet above their bed, nearly reaching the vigas on the ceiling, the sheets still wrapped around their legs and dangling down.

I ran from the sight. It scared me. But I never thought it was anything other than a mechanical contraption, probably of my mother's devising, to enhance their love-making. I supposed when you're in your forties you needed all the help you can get. My parents raised me to be a true skeptic. There's nothing I believe without unequivocal proof, even my dear mother and father. I never violated their privacy again no matter how bad curiosity had bit me.

I glance up at the crèche that was my mother's on the narrow ledge above the hive-shaped adobe hearth. It is the only item I possess to mark Christmas. They are just an ordinary family fallen on hard times, to me, but they are held together by their love and they will make it.

I laugh recalling my first serious boyfriend Edward's coming over here at Christmas six years ago. He told me the crèche was idolatry and my little live-potted Xmas tree was a pagan symbol used to invoke the devil. What a spoilsport. How to put a damp blanket on Christmas cheer.

"How about gingerbread men?" I asked him. "Does it promote cannibalism, you know, like the Last Supper?"

"Don't be ridiculous, Hypatia. You need to call on Jesus and beg His forgiveness."

"The hell with Jesus and the ass he rode in on," I told him.

Edward sputtered as though all the circuits in his brain were misfiring. He never got the words out. I grabbed his coat from a peg by the front door and threw it down the walkway after him. It landed in a puddle of slush: not my intention, but I wasn't sorry, either. What a drip.

I get up to make a cup of ginger tea with honey. It is only four o'clock and the sun is already setting. I remember what one of the old horsemen from the Pueblo said about the white man and Daylight Savings Time. He remarked it was like cutting one end off a blanket and sewing onto the opposite end to make it longer.

I pull my favorite chair in the parlor nearer the fire. Recalling boyfriends seems to be the theme of the evening. I take a sip of tea and give the perpetual log a little poke simply out of habit. It perks up a bit and I nestle into the chair.

Feeling I had learned my lesson dating a Christian, I found it easy to fall for Ephraim, a Jew from Santa Fe whose parents wrote a three-volume set on the Diaspora in New Mexico. At least he could quote a few things not in the Talmud. He was a sweet man who didn't push his religion. I found other things to do on his Sabbath. But his dietary proscriptions drove me crazy.

Like a devoted girlfriend, I learned to cook according to his requirements, not that it occurred to me he might accommodate himself to a couple of my customs. That year I went all-out making and baking the Christmas foods I remembered as a girl, but done according to his religion—mostly. I liked Ephraim a lot, even if actual love was still on the back burner.

"What are these tiny red specks in the scalloped potatoes, Hypatia?" he asked.

"Small bits of bacon," I told him.

"Bacon!" he screamed.

"Let loose a little, Ephraim. It's Christmas. Besides, I'm pretty sure it's kosher bacon."

"Kosher bacon? Are you trying to send me to *Gehinnom*?"

I stood up and slammed down the casserole baking dish so hard it cracked in half. I nudged Ephraim up out of his chair and escorted him by the elbow to the front door.

"No, just trying to get you out my house and out of my life. Your going to purgatory is up to Jehovah and, from what I read, he doesn't like anybody. He's a mean old white man with hemorrhoids and an electric finger."

I flung his jacket after him, knocking his yarmulke, his beanie, into a half-melted puddle. Well, maybe I'd been aiming that time.

In the last of the day's light I see it is snowing lightly: big, fluffy flakes. It is supposed to develop into a fairly strong storm with a foot of snow possible by morning. I am glad I have nowhere to go tonight, though I wouldn't mind if someone visited me.

With boyfriend Number Three, I eschewed Christians and Jews, and sidestepped Muslims and Mormons, and went straight for a born-again atheist. I consulted an analyst for my depression and sorry love-life, but it developed rather quickly into something more. I thought it might be unethical, but the doctor assured me no one would know. I wasn't quite sure what that had to do with my therapy.

Dr. Egad De Bockel came to Red Willow a decade before from Holland and set up his practice to serve well-heeled clients— as in high-heels. They came here from the big cities in Colorado, Texas, and California. He assured me I was living in a "hat-sized fable" and that I could have any man I put my mind to wanting, even him.

Egad was a far better lover than either Edward or Ephraim, and he treated me as though I were special to him in ways beyond mere doctor-patient. I was naive back then and fell in love with his handsome goatee which he employed to tickle me into howling ecstasy.

Dr. De Bockel did not believe in God, but he had his own religion of psychiatry in which everything I did meant something else. I started saying the opposite of what I intended in hopes he might mistakenly take it the right way. I became so tangled in knots and subterfuges that I thought of seeing another analyst to get myself sorted out, but it felt like cheating.

The break-up with Egad happened once more on Christmas Eve. He questioned why I had a little tree with lights in the parlor.

"That tree is a symbol of gross capitalistic commercialism.

It doesn't belong in the home of any sane person who doesn't believe in fairy stories," he chortled.

"Listen, you affected windbag," I replied, "that gross commercialism pays your way. If not for capitalism, there'd be no one with money to fritter away on getting analyzed, that's for sure. They'd have to consult a genuine witch doctor who'd at least shrink their heads for real."

Dr. De Bockel huffed and puffed and swelled himself up like an indignant blowfish. He stormed out the front door. Halfway down the walk, he turned for his tweedy little hat. I tossed it to him like a frisbee. The hat circled around his head and plopped in a patch of mud. I hadn't meant it, but that did nothing to keep me from laughing hysterically.

<hr>

It appears I will have to spend this Christmas alone. I decide to soothe myself with a hot bubble bath and a second cup of ginger tea. The instant I turn off the tap, ready to climb in, I hear a crash from the living room that sounds like the perpetual log tumbling out of the fireplace. I grab my bathrobe from the hook and go to investigate.

Soot fans out from the hearth. I discover a plate of sugar cookies and glass of milk sitting on the coffee table. It has to be Weird Santa. He's got it ass-backwards.

He's left a package in luminescent paper beside the hearth. The fire feels good. I hold the present against my breasts and turn around to warm my backside. I pull at the illuminated ribbon. The present puffs up several times in size but remains flat. It feels like heavy fabric or leather.

What tumbles from the neon paper is what appears to be a vinyl pool inflatable in the shape of a man. I stretch it to its full length: about six feet, anatomically correct. It makes me laugh. The laughter feels good on Christmas Eve. I guess I got my wish after all.

"Merry Christmas, Weird Santa," I holler up the flue, knowing he went to a bit of trouble to make it look like that's how he'd come and gone.

The inflatable is a sickly pinkish color, not quite opaque, and he's a ginger. The valve is where you might expect. Naughty old Santa. The foreskin is the valve cap. I laugh so hard I cannot get any air into my new blow-up beau.

Sitting down on the sofa, I stare at the fire and reminisce. I revisit my memory of Number Four, the tortured Goth poet too frail to consider manual labor, which he saw as demeaning. He affected to be the Edgar Allen Ginsberg of Goth poetry. His poems, all the rage among the trust-fund hippies of Red Willow, were depressing. He was depressing.

We spent Christmas Eve together two years ago, the year before Elliot. I came home late after staying to help my friend Ginnie in her punk jewelry boutique. Edgar sat in the parlor stark naked, all but tapping his foot with impatience.

"Where were you?" he asked, glowering.

"Earning our daily bread, dearest. Ginnie stayed open late. We had customers."

Edgar stood up, growing erect, and motioned me to my knees. I was in no mood. I hoped his ass was getting cold. I put my lips around the tip of his penis.

"You are an imbecile, Hypatia. You are so literal. *Blow job* is just an expression, an idiom. What do you think will be accomplished by blowing?"

"That I'd get out of having to give you a blow job, you jerk. Out. Right now."

I pushed him by degrees toward the front door and opened it.

"Hypatia, are you crazy? It's snowing."

I gave him a playful push and he sprawled in an icy puddle. Before he could scramble back up the walkway, I flung his car keys at him and wished him a Happy Holiday. Pulling the blinds helped conserve heat. I donated his clothes to the homeless shelter.

I light the old railroad lantern that had been my father's. It casts a cheering glow. Weird Santa's Yule log flares a little. I feel sleepy, and light-headed from blowing up the mannikin. It is nearly fully inflated. I set him on the floor and lie down on my back near the fire, putting my head against his belly. Feeling comfy and warm, I fall asleep, wishing I had wished to see my parents again instead.

———————◦——————

I awake startled and gasping for air. The Inflatable Man has moved, or at least it seemed like it in my half-wakeful state. I must have poked a hole in him. I hear a leak, like a sigh. I turn around. His chest heaves slowly and rhythmically. This is one re-alistic toy. I wonder where Weird Santa got it. Ginnie would get a hoot out of having one.

The blow-up dummy's eyes open and it sits up. I jump up and grab the poker, brandishing it like Hypatia the Amazon. He does not seem the least bit threatened.

"All right, buster, get up. Move slowly or I'll bash your head in."

"Why do wish to hurt me, Hypatia? I am your Christmas present. Don't you want to play with me before you break me?"

It turns its head and looks at me. I lean forward and rest my hand on its shoulder. It is warm and firm, not like a hollow man, a balloon man. It must be a robotic toy. *But how did it come all flat and folded up like that?* I wonder.

"You breathed life into me," it says in a beautiful baritone. "Now I am yours."

Yeah, in my dreams, I think.

"But you are awake," it says.

"Oh, so, a toy that reads minds," I beam at it.

"I am not a toy. I am a man."

His penis swells and inches upward.

"Did Weird Santa send you?"

"Santa Nicolás brought me, yes, but you breathed life into me. I am yours."

What is going on? I ask myself.

"It is Christmas. I am your present. Let's be friends."

He sounds like a *Forrest Gump* simpleton.

"I find it hard to believe in Christmas. It's mostly for children," I tell him.

"Then be a child, Hypatia."

"Please don't tell me what to do, uh… uh… What's your name?"

"I don't have one until you give me a name."

I think for a minute. It will most definitely not begin with the letter "E."

"How about 'Number Six,'" I suggest. "'Six' for short."

"I am Six," he says, beaming with pride.

His voice reminds me of a cello: resonant, deep, and sad. His beautiful, rugged body distracts me so that I can no longer concentrate on keeping straight what's real and what isn't. I tell him to sit by the fire while I look for something of Elliot's to hang on Six's well-built frame.

I open the bottom drawers of the chest where Elliot kept some of his old clothes, hoping I might have overlooked something. He was about the same size. There's a worn pair of Levi's and a threadbare gray gym sweatshirt. I just hope nothing rubs off. I like Six just as he is.

Six gets into the jeans and sweatshirt, and I swear he is almost as sexy with his clothes on. We lie opposite each other on the sofa and wiggle our bare feet beneath the cushions. Six pulls a slightly tattered blanket over us. It has one end cut off and sewn coarsely to the other.

"Where did this come from, Six?"

"I guess it must be my baby blanket," he says, breaking into a grin.

"There's something you're not telling me."

"I am the gift, you are the recipient, Santa Nicolás is the messenger, and your parents are the givers."

"You saw them?"

"No, not actually, but they send you their love. They have sent me to you as an expression of their love. I am your present. I am yours now, all yours."

I am too tired to argue or probe further. Moving to lie next to him, I snuggle against his chest. Six wraps his arms around me. Knowing he came from my parents, I feel comfortable and safe. I fall asleep listening to his heartbeat.

———————————⊃◦⊂———————————

I awake alone, tangled in the tattered blanket. The sofa is not the best place for a long lie-down. I knew it had to be a dream, and feel sorry that someone like Six is not real. I smell bacon frying and sit bolt upright on the lumpy sofa. There is clattering in the kitchen.

Six is at the stove frying bacon and making a large omelet with jalapeños and cheese. Bread pops up from the toaster, and he reaches for butter and cherry jam. He senses my standing there and turns around, switching on his smile.

"Merry Christmas, Hypatia. Are you hungry?"

"I'm famished."

"Go sit down. I'll bring it to the table."

He pours a mug of coffee and, adding a splash of cream, hands it to me. Somehow he knows how I like my coffee. He brings a tray with two plates of toast, omelet, and three strips of bacon each. He seems amused by my voracious appetite, watching me intently as I devour each mouthful. We discuss plans for a Christmas supper and manage to agree on everything. I'm sure the real Six will turn up sooner or later, the one with the horns.

After breakfast, he hurries off with the dishes. He begins washing them and I point out to him there is a dishwasher.

"I do not know how to operate one," he tells me. "Do you need a license?"

"My ex seemed to think so, but, no, you don't need a license as long as it stays in the house."

He doesn't realize I'm joking. I find his innocence endearing somehow. I head off to the bathroom. The bubble bath has long ago gone flat and cold. I decide to have a long shower instead, for as long as the meager hot water holds out.

I shut my eyes and let the soothing water stream over my face. *Ahh.* When I open them again, Six is peeking around the shower curtain, smiling at me.

"Why don't you hop in?" I tell him. "No. Take your clothes off first."

"Right," he says.

Six's skin is less puckered. He has filled out nicely and his flesh tone looks more natural. It is browner. His hair, too, is now more auburn. He is quite a specimen of manhood.

Six steps into the shower and giggles like a boy. He wiggles around and tries to get behind me.

"It tickles," he howls.

I wouldn't be surprised if it were his first shower. The water seems to bring out his "new" smell, like something starched or sized when it gets wet. I show him how to adjust the stream by turning the showerhead. I have never known a man willing, even eager, to learn something from a woman. It's a first. He thanks me. Am I dreaming now? I don't know whether to stick myself or him with a pin. Will I wake up? Will he deflate?

Six takes the washcloth and soap from me and begins washing my breasts. He lets the washcloth drop and continues with just his hands and the bar of soap. It is exhilarating, then exciting. He washes me everywhere, slowly, caressingly. He tilts my head back and shampoos my hair, running his fingers through it, pulling me back beneath the water to rinse me off.

"Your turn," I say.

As soon as I touch him with the soapy rag, he laughs. He jumps around so much I could hold the washcloth still and let him do the work. I think the soap has gotten rid of that "new man" smell. When I cup his penis in my soapy hands, his little friend wakes from his slumber.

Six lifts me by my waist and I put my arms around his neck and wrap my legs around his hips. Despite the slightly awkward position, he enters me with ease. His movements are masterful: no need for instruction here. He knows precisely what I want. He has the loping grace and rhythm of a cat, of a mountain lion.

At the moment of our shared climax, the shower grows noticeably warmer, steamy hot. I experience an orgasm throughout my body, everywhere Six has touched me, everywhere the water flows, from my ears to my toes. I look deep into his eyes.

"It is hard to breathe," he says.

"Yes, that happens," I tell him. "Next time, we'll go a little slower."

After our shower, Six enfolds me in a warm towel and rubs me dry. I scurry off to the bedroom. The house feels chilly after the hot shower. *Where'd he get a warm towel?* I wonder. The man is full of mysteries.

I get dressed in a green skirt, white blouse, and red sweater, going intentionally sappy for Christmas. I find a pair of stretched-out old wool hiking socks for Six. He's in the kitchen preparing the supper we'd discussed, dressed again in the old jeans and sweatshirt. I hand him the oversized socks. He puts them on, then goes back to stirring something in a saucepan.

All the supper choices are mine except one. Six wanted to make gingerbread cookies. He's a gentle and agreeable man. I hope I'm not railroading him.

"Tomorrow we have to get you boots and a jacket," I tell him. "And gloves."

"That would be nice," he says.

"Sure it would when I'm the one paying," I grouse.

"I came here with nothing. I came here empty, Hypatia. These are not even my clothes. You gave me everything and you filled me up. I have only myself to give you."

I put my arms around him and cry into his shoulder.

"I did not mean to be so mean, Six. I'm sorry, especially on Christmas."

He wipes my tears with his thumbs.

"It is time for the gingerbread men to be born," he says.

He opens the oven and grabs the cookie sheet with his bare hand. I scream, but he does not seem hurt and does not react to my loud cry. Instead, he smiles. Maybe he thinks it was a squeal of delight. He certainly has a high tolerance for heat.

The aroma of gingerbread made with real ginger returns me to girlhood. Six scoops white frosting into a pastry bag, twists it closed, and hands it to me. I begin decorating the gingerbread men. I give them tiny male appendages. Six laughs. I have not had this much fun at Christmas since my parents went away.

When I've put icing on roughly half the cookies, Six takes the pastry bag from me and decorates the remaining asexual ones.

These he gives sugary breasts and little vaginal "V"s.

"If I put the cookie sheets back in the oven, maybe we'll get a bunch of gingerbread kids," he suggests.

It is his first intentional joke. Six hands me a steaming mug of ginger tea—prepared when I wasn't paying attention—and waves me toward the parlor.

A second squall of snow has begun, already a few inches, yet the flagstone walkway is perfectly clear. I ask Six when he shoveled.

"After our shower and before making supper," he tells me.

"But the walkway is still dry."

"It must still be warm."

"Warm?" I ask him.

"Here, taste this," he remarks, putting a spoon to my lips.

I don't know if he's trying to distract me or really wants to know what I think of his sauce for the scalloped potatoes. In either case it worked. It's delicious. I return to my mug of tea. I feel like a child again: warm and cozy and cared for. It is my fervent wish not to have to send Six down the walkway on Christmas—or any other day.

———————

I awaken from my doze. Six stands at the hearth. He hears me and turns around. The perpetual Yule log flares up even though he has no tools in his hands and the screen is closed. The wind moans. I become engulfed in scrumptious aromas, each of them distinct, and breathe them in.

"Come, Hypatia. Our meal is ready," he says, offering me a hand to get up from the sofa.

I open the oven and peek at the beautifully crisped roast duckling. The orange and honey sauce bubbles on a back burner. The casserole dish of scalloped potatoes garnished with bits of bacon and parsley sits on the tile counter. A loaf of bread, bursting from its pan, sits on the cutting board.

"Have a seat," Six tells me. "Let me serve you."

He brings in bowls and platters of food, including a perfectly carved duck. He sits down across from me in the dining area, his chest puffed out with pride.

"It is beautiful, Six," I tell him. "Oh, don't forget the candles."

As I scoot my chair closer, I see a flash at the corner of my eye. Six is withdrawing his finger from the now-burning candle.

"You lit that with your finger," I tell him more than ask him.

"Yes," he admits.

"And the Yule log and the hot shower and the walkway and the towel?"

"Yes, yes, yes, yes."

"How do you do it?"

"I don't know," he replies. "But I can't keep supper warm forever. You must say a thanksgiving. It is customary."

"Why me?"

"We are beneath your roof."

I am speechless, a condition my father believed impossible. Many impossible things happen at Christmas, I guess, and if they happen then they must be possible.

"I thank my parents, Oscar and Hildegard, for building this roof over our heads, for providing this wonderful meal with the proceeds from stock sales, but most of all for the man they sent me who made every tidbit and morsel with love. And Merry Christmas to Weird Santa Nicolás, too, whoever he is."

Six touches my lips with his finger.

"Thank you," he says, and scoops a heap of steaming potatoes onto my plate.

Throughout the meal I glance past Six at the gingerbread people on their cookie sheets on the tile counter behind him, basking like naked sunbathers. I couldn't possibly bite off an arm or a leg or a head. I plot to save them.

"Why don't we get a little Christmas tree tomorrow?" I suggest. "They'll probably be free, since it will be the day after. We'll cut our own."

"That would be fun," Six replies, licking orange sauce from his fingers.

"I'll get red and green ribbon and we'll hang the gingerbread cookies on the tree," I add.

"OK," he agrees. "Then we can admire them every evening with a glass of milk after supper."

I laugh. If Six learns any faster, I may find it hard to keep up with him.

NEVER TOO OLD, NEVER TOO LATE

I am happy to have the company of Phaedre, my neighbor, on the long subway ride to and from the farmers' market down on Union Square. She is also my friend, a red-haired young woman from Ireland. I'm a gray-haired old *babushka* from what was once Russia and then became the Soviet Union and now is Russia again. I lived through it all.

My family and I—my brother Nikolai, my daughter Moosha, and my grandchildren Maxim and Nina—arrived in New York after the collapse of the USSR six years ago. I'd dreamed of coming to America my entire life. I'm glad I learned patience as a child. I am now eighty-two years old and still in no hurry. My friend is also patient. I get along with her better than my own daughter, though Phaedre is closer in age to my granddaughter.

Phaedre and I do not attempt to be heard above the screeching and whooshing of the A train when it goes express after leaving our neighborhood in Washington Heights. We do not talk again until it reaches Harlem at 125th Street.

"My grandson speaks of you often, Phaedre. I believe he is falling down for you."

"The expression is just plain old *falling for someone*, Ana," she tells me, smiling. "I would not complain if he has fallen for me. Did you by any chance cast a spell on him?"

"Not a very strong one, my child, more like steering something rather than pushing it along. My recipes are gentle. I try to be kind."

"I understand, Ana," she says. "I just want to be sure his falling for me is Maxim's idea."

"It is certainly Max's idea, dear. But he hesitates. He wastes time. He can't decide. I'm not so much putting a spell on him as I am dispelling the fog he finds himself in."

An old fellow comes up to me and Phaedre, weaving and bobbing as the train lurches. He holds out his hand and I put the coins from my pocket in his dirty palm. He looks down at me and thanks me, offering me God's blessing.

"Thank you," I tell him. "I need all the help I can get."

Phaedre and I emerge from the *Metró*, the subway, at Union Square and Sixteenth Street. The market is crowded today, despite the cold and the snow earlier in the week. It is the last Friday market before Christmas. It is Christmas Eve. Phaedre takes my elbow so we do not get separated.

My eyes twirl inside my head there is so much to see. My nose twitches, inhaling all the aromas: bread and cookies, soup and coffee and tea, and the enormous potted pine trees encircling the park. My ears tingle, too, taking in the tinkling bells, the Christmas music over the loudspeakers, and the chatter of passing conversations in more languages than even I understand.

Faces are rosy and smiling; vendors are eager to please their customers. We stop at Mr. Arkady's poultry stall. He winks at us.

"Pretty fresh today," he says. "And I don't need ice."

"Do you have any live hens today?" I ask him.

"No, Miss Ana. The health department said it wasn't allowed, that chickens are dirty birds. So, I asked him, what about pigeons? Are the pigeons so clean? I don't see you chasing down pigeons. He had no answer for that."

"Well, then, two dead hens, Mr. Arkady," I tell him. "Perhaps there will be less fuss if I do not bring a live chicken on the subway train."

Phaedre laughs.

"It caused quite a commotion when it got loose, Mr. Arkady," she tells him. "Perhaps you wouldn't mind keeping our parcels until we head home. We have other shopping to do."

"Certainly," he tells my friend, handing her our receipts.

We walk on. I have to be careful. There are many icy spots. Phaedre gives me her arm.

Pine trees in their burlap-covered root-balls encircle most of the square. They are decorated for Christmas with multi-colored ornaments and tiny white lights. They blot out most of the buildings surrounding Union Square, making it seem that I am once more back at the winter market in Odessa.

I stand still. Phaedre stops beside me. I close my eyes a moment.

The fragrance of the pine trees transports me back to Russia. I am a young girl again, during the Great War in Europe and before the Revolution. My older brother, Nikolai, says something to me, but my mind has been wandering. I open my eyes again.

Nikolai and I stand in the middle of the Odessa market. It is cold and the snow is piled up. There are very few merchants or customers.

"Could you listen to me for once, Ana.," my brother says. "Our neighbors say it was definitely a police wagon that took mother and father away. I went to the local constabulary, but they will tell me nothing. They laughed at me, called me a disloyal son to lose track of my parents. They are the sort of imbecilic bureaucrats that will have no place after the Revolution."

I don't know what more to suggest to Nikolai. We have tried everything we know how to do to locate our parents. We pawned one of our mother's amber bracelets to bribe a guard at the local prison. He took the bribe but failed to deliver any information on Catherine and Leon Mendeleyev. He, too, heaped derisive laughter on our heads. Nikolai said the guard was the sort of dishonest official that will be lined up before a firing squad once the Revolution does away with corruption.

Nikolai has gone from banishing those he dislikes to executing them within the course of a single conversation. Though I am only eight years old, I do not understand how the Revolution will be an improvement on anything.

"Ana, Ana," a voice says, startling me. "Are you all right?"

I know the voice. Someone tugs at my coat sleeve. I open

my eyes. I am back in Union Square. It is my friend, Phaedre.

"Sorry, dear," I tell her. "Sometimes I weave in and out, back and forth, between here and there."

"Where is there, Ana?"

"The Old Country," I tell her. "My parents' house in Odessa. I remember them always at Christmas. The smell of pine boughs takes me back there."

"That is so sweet," Phaedre remarks.

"I am afraid my other association with Christmas, dear child, is that my parents were arrested by the Tsar's police just before Christmas in 1916, over seventy years ago. I have not seen them since."

"Oh, I am so sorry for you, Ana."

"That is how life works, child. There's always a bit of sorrow in our happiness, and a speck of joy in our sadness. Come. We'll stay warmer if we keep moving."

Phaedre takes hold of my elbow again even though this section of the walkway, receiving all of the afternoon sun, is ice-free.

"Oh, do you smell that, Phaedre? It makes my mouth water. The baker must have just taken something out of his little electric oven. Let's go see."

We hurry over to Hoffman's Fine Baked Goods. This time he has set up next to the tea and coffee vendor—a fine idea.

"There you are, Ana," Hoffman tells me. "I expected you 'round about now. I just took your special order out of the oven."

"Phaedre, dear, please do not look. One of the items is for you. We'll go next door and order our tea, Mr. Hoffman. When my items are cool, you may wrap them up individually. Don't forget to mark the names on them."

"I won't, Ana. Is there anything you ladies would like to have with your tea when you return?"

"How about two crescent rolls, Mr. Hoffman. Is that all right with you, Phaedre?"

My friend agrees. Hoffman places our croissants inside his little oven to warm them up. When we return with our paper cups of tea, the pastries are hot enough to melt butter. I pay him for our rolls and for my custom order. I hand one of the oddly-shaped little parcels, wrapped in white paper, to Phaedre.

"What's this?" she asks.

"It's your Christmas present a day early, child."

"But it says 'Maxim' on it."

"Yes, I know, dear. He'll get the one marked 'Phaedre.'"

"Oh, look," she declares. "You've got ones for my cousin, Fitzgerald, and his partner, Antonio, too. How sweet of you, Ana. Isn't there one for Nina?"

"No, she's not yet old enough to have someone special in her life. My granddaughter will receive something else, something just for her."

"You've intrigued me, Ana," Phaedre says. "May I peek at my present?"

Hoffman stands at the counter, waiting to see my neighbor's reaction.

"You may take a peek, Phaedre," I tell her, "but you may not eat the cookie until tomorrow. It has to be eaten on Christmas Day. They are magic cookies."

"Oh, my God. Ana. Mr. Hoffman. It is gorgeous. I couldn't possibly eat a gingerbread cookie that looks like Max. It's exactly how he combs his hair and how he wears his glasses: a little bit crooked. I will save it and put him on the Christmas tree—when we get one, that is."

"You mustn't save the cookie, Phaedre. You and Max must eat each other up. Mr. Hoffman has baked them according to my exact recipe and instructions."

"Of course, Ana, I will do as you say," Phaedre tells me, smiling as one humors an old woman, an eccentric old woman.

She accepts the small brown paper shopping bag from Hoffman containing the other three gingerbread cookies. I don't know whether Hoffman believes they are magic cookies, either, but he has never skimped on the ingredients or failed to follow my recipes to the letter.

"All right, Phaedre," I tell my grandson's girlfriend. "Time to put Max back in his paper. You must not let him see it and, even if he wants to show you his cookie of you, you must not look. You must simply gobble each other up."

"Does that go for my cousin Fitz and his boyfriend Antonio, too?" she asks.

"Yes, child. Love is love."

Phaedre wraps my "grandson" back in his paper and places him inside the brown bag.

"Good-bye, Mr. Hoffman," I tell him. "Thank you. And Happy Chanukah."

"And a Merry Christmas to you and your friend."

I nod to him and continue down the path with Phaedre. When we have finished our tea, she offers to discard our paper cups in the trash.

"No, dear. I have a use for them."

She watches me intently. Removing my mitten, I scoop dirt from one of the potted pine trees into each of the cups. Then I pinch off a tiny bud-bearing branch and use it to poke a hole in the plastic lid. I push the little cutting deep into the dirt.

"One for you and Max, one for Fitzgerald and Antonio."

"Thank you, Ana."

Phaedre puts the coffee cups containing the tiny pine cuttings into the little shopping bag with the cookies. She is a good-hearted neighbor and friend. I am happy she and my grandson have found each other. I believe they will make each other happy for the rest of their lives.

The sun is setting at the end of the long canyon of Fifteenth Street. All the buildings look like reddish stone, like the sandstone buildings in Odessa.

"I'm looking for the fellow who sells candy, Phaedre. Have you seen him? I'm looking for the little white candy beads they sprinkle on nonpareils."

"I haven't seen him yet, Ana, but we haven't been down this path," she tells me, pointing.

The air grows chillier even though the sunset has suffused it with a warm, rosy glow.

"There he is," she says. "Be careful of this icy patch."

Mr. Collins has decorated his stall with a festive Yuletide banner and two enormous striped candy-canes.

"My dear, Ana," he says to me. "It is always nice to see you.

Merry Christmas."

"Likewise, Mr. Collins. I am looking for the tiny sugar beads they sprinkle on chocolate nonpareils. Just the beads, if you please."

"Hmm," he says, stroking his gray beard.

Collins nods to Phaedre as he takes a plastic box from beneath the counter of his stall. The box contains many little drawers. He opens several before finding what he wants.

"Here we are," he tells me. "The package is opened. This is all I have left. Excuse me a moment."

The candyman waits on a customer interested in bark candy and a box of hand-dipped chocolates. He takes her money and packs up her purchase.

"Now," he says, returning to me and holding up the opened cellophane bag of white sugary beads.

"That will do just fine, Mr. Collins. What do I owe you for the candy beads?" I ask him.

"It's too small an amount to charge you, Ana. Merry Christmas."

"Same to you, Mr. Collins. Thank you."

Phaedre and I find a bench from which most of the snow has been brushed off. We sit down and I pull off my mittens. I take the bag of sugar beads from my pocket and, reaching over, sprinkle them into the shopping bag my friend has placed on the ground between us. She looks at me questioningly.

"Tiny ornaments for the tiny trees," I tell her.

"Of course," she says, laughing. "You are so inventive, Ana. You seem to really enjoy Christmas."

"Yes, very much. It has always been my favorite time of the year, despite many unpleasant memories that got tacked onto the holiday."

Phaedre looks down into the bag.

"The sugar beads have all stuck to the pine needles, Ana. They look like tiny Christmas ornaments."

"I was hoping they would," I tell her. "My parents preferred simple decorations for our Christmas trees."

"Were you ever able to find out what happened to them, Ana?"

"The Ministry of Prisons told me that, as my parents and other prisoners were being transported to Irkutsk in Siberia, the train was derailed by members of the Revolutionary Guard. Most of the passengers were killed. My parents' bodies were never recovered."

"Oh, how terrible," my friend tells me.

"Not at all," I reply. "You have to understand Russian bureaucratese. It can be taken whatever way you please. I took it to mean that their bodies were never recovered because they had escaped. I am hopeful my parents and I will meet again before I am gone. That is my Christmas wish this year, as it has been every year since my parents disappeared."

"But how old would they be?" Phaedre asks, helping me up from the park bench.

I take her hand, squinting my eyes to do a bit of calculation.

"They'd be a hundred-and-two, dear. Certainly not too old. It's quite possible this is the year I shall see them one last time."

Phaedre squeezes my hand. It comforts me. She is such a kind person. My grandson is very lucky. Phaedre and I start walking.

"Oh, there," I say. "The fabric remnants. I see something for my daughter, Moosha. The brocaded sofa pillows. Would you be able to carry them home?"

"Yes, of course," she replies.

We approach Mr. Finkelstein. He remembers me.

"Happy Christmas, Miss Ana. What has caught your eye?"

"The white pillows," I tell him. "The ones with the gold tassels."

"Those are the only pillows I have today."

"Then they shall have to do," I remark.

We chuckle. Phaedre joins in.

"And for you, Ana, a special price in honor of Christmas and Chanukah," Finkelstein says.

He figures on a small pad of paper. He does more calculating than was involved in Mr. Einstein's equations. He quotes me a price and I wrinkle my nose.

"Look, Miss Ana. I don't want to pack them up and take

them home again. Make me a reasonable offer and they are yours."

"Of course it will be a reasonable offer, Mr. Finkelstein. I wouldn't waste your time with an unreasonable offer, would I? Five dollars for the pair."

"All right. All right," Finkelstein says, holding up his palms. "But only because it is Christmas and Chanukah and it is late in the day—and because I like you."

"Deal," I tell him, counting out the money from my change purse.

Finkelstein pushes the pillows into an oversized plastic bag, the kind that fits in a trash can. He draws the strings and hands the bag to Phaedre. I take the paper bag containing the pine cuttings and the gingerbread cookies from her. We wish Finkelstein a Merry Christmas and he wishes us a Happy Chanukah.

"Yes, dear," I tell Phaedre. "I know what you are thinking. They are the ugliest sofa pillows in all of creation. Moosha will love them."

She laughs. I put the paper shopping bag in my right hand. Phaedre slings the plastic bag with the throw pillows over her shoulder like Father Frost with his sack of presents. She latches onto my left arm.

"Only two more items," I tell her. "Something for my brother and a gift for Nina. I think she would like a piece of jewelry. I wonder if Mr. Ordoubadi is here today. It's getting late."

"And snowing again," Phaedre remarks. "We have not gone this way," she suggests.

Ordoubadi's booth is at the end of the walk near the Park Avenue side of Union Square. His banner announces "Fine Jewelry from Around the World," listing all seven continents and the nine planets below that. He has a handmade sign wishing Happy Kwanza.

Ordoubadi is not behind the counter of his stall. Instead, there is an old couple in their hooded winter coats, shawls, and knit caps, slouched forward in their lawn chairs, snoring. As one breathes in, the other breathes out, making their gentle racket continuous.

Not wishing to disturb them, Phaedre and I examine the

jewelry on their black velvet trays on the counter. The snowflakes land on the velvet, pausing a moment before vanishing. Phaedre points to a small but flashy bracelet made of what appears to be polished amber. My mother had a similar piece on her wrist when the Tsar's police clamped manacles on her.

An strange swirl of heavy snow descends out of nowhere, making it hard to see. The old couple stirs and, stooped over, come to the counter. All I can see are their eyes, noses, and smiling mouths—no foreheads or chins. The snow stops abruptly.

"May we help you, young lady," the old woman asks, grinning.

I think she is talking to Phaedre, but they look straight at me. I laugh.

"Yes, we mean you, Ana," the old man says.

They pull back their fur-fringed hoods and remove their knit caps. Though there are many layers of wrinkles and furrows, I recognize them by their dazzling blue eyes.

"Mother. Father," I say, the words catching in my throat. My heart races and I feel dizzy.

I drop my shopping bag. Phaedre leans the bag of pillows against the counter and puts her arm around me, steadying me. I cannot see for the tears filling my eyes, nor speak for choking on the words.

My parents' smiles tell me all I wish to know. They converse with me in Russian.

"Yes, daughter, it has been a long time of many winters and many hardships. We are here in answer to you Christmas wish. Merry Christmas, Ana."

My parents come from behind the counter and wrap their arms around me, encircling me with hugs and warmth. They are much shorter than I remember. We cry tears of sorrow and weep for joy.

I show them I still carry my lucky rabbit's foot from my girlhood.

"I never lost hope," I say.

"Nor did we, child. Please introduce us to your friend, Ana," my father says in English. His voice is still strong, but the cold has made it brittle.

"This is my friend and neighbor, Phaedre McGuirk. She will soon be engaged to marry your great-grandson Maxim Andreyevich."

"I believe Max has to propose to me first, Ana," Phaedre says, chuckling.

"Oh, he will do so quite soon, child," I assure her. "Perhaps as early as tomorrow."

"Are you both really here?" Phaedre asks my mother and father. "Or has your daughter put a spell on me?"

"We are mostly here," my father tells her. "A little less than most people, but quite a bit more than some."

"I see," she replies, though I doubt she does.

"We will have to return home soon, Ana. Were you interested in my polished amber bracelet, dear?" my mother asks me.

"Yes, Mama. I remember it fondly. I'd like your great-granddaughter, Nina, to have it. I recognized the bracelet before I recognized you."

"It has changed less," she says, smiling a beautiful, shining, happy smile. "You may have it, Ana. We have no need of money. Take darling Nina our blessings."

"I will," I promise.

My mother places her amber bracelet and the matching amber ring in a tiny muslin bag and ties the drawstring. I accept it from her with a deep bow.

"We have a letter for Nikolai. Please give it to him with our love, Ana," my father says.

"Yes, Papa, I will. Thank you. I know my brother will not believe I have spoken with you, even with my neighbor as witness."

I put the tiny cloth bag of jewelry and the letter for Nikolai in my coat pocket.

"We must go, dear Ana. We are so very tired," my mother says.

"It is quite exhausting standing in two places at once," my father adds.

My parents kiss me on both cheeks and I return their

embraces. Our cheeks are salty with tears. They touch Phaedre's hand, but she does not seem to feel it. They grow thin, wispy, like the steam of our breath disappearing into the frigid air.

My friend stands with her mouth agape, her eyes wide.

"They just vanished," she says, her voice quivering. "Like mist."

"Yes, I know, child. The magic recipe that brought my mother and father here works for only a short time. My heart is glad. I am grateful I saw them one more time before they left this world."

"But it's very startling to someone who doesn't believe in magic," Phaedre says.

"Perhaps now you believe a little bit more?"

"Yes, but I'm still confused."

"Confusion is a condition of life, child, with or without magic," I tell her. She smiles and takes my hand.

"Come," I tell her. "We still have to stop by Mr. Arkady to pick up our chickens. It is getting late. Our families will be eager to see us."

The butcher hands Phaedre the paper shopping bag containing our chickens. He has wrapped cardboard around the handles to make it easier for her to carry. She slings the plastic bag with the ugly pillows over her other shoulder and takes the drawstrings.

I carry the bag with the gingerbread cookies and miniature Christmas trees, taking hold of Phaedre's elbow with my left hand. We walk to the *Metró* station at Fourteenth Street. We take the handicapped elevator at street level down to the subway platform. We must ride the L train over to Eighth Avenue to catch the A train. We carry on our conversation between the racket of arriving and departing trains.

"Since you and Max will be having supper with Fitzgerald and Antonio tomorrow at your apartment, I shall leave all four of the gingerbread cookies with you, my dear. I'll explain what each of you must do. You must not get it wrong or the magic in the cookies will not work."

"I shall pay close attention, Ana. I promise."

"God bless you, child," I tell her. "I shall explain how to care for the baby Christmas trees, too. I hope that the other little gift I have for you will come in handy—just in case," I say, patting her hand.

———————⊃◦⊂———————

When her cousin Fitz and his companion, Antonio, leave Phaedre's basement apartment on Ft. Washington Avenue, she and Maxim kiss each other with a bit more passion than they felt comfortable expressing in front of their friends.

"That was a fine Christmas supper, Phaedre," Max tells her, kissing her again.

"Don't forget the food Fitz and Antonio brought."

"Believe me, I haven't. Their *chile rellenos* were incredibly tasty, but a bit too spicy for my Russian tongue."

"You'll get used to it, Max. New York comes in so many flavors. What do you say we get the clean-up out of the way? I can't wait to open the magic cookie from your grandma."

"I'm sorry you've had to listen to her nonsense, Phaedre. It's not enough she bothers her family with her magic formulas."

He puts the bones of the chicken carcass in the garbage can beneath the sink. They are picked clean.

"I love your grandma, Max. It's not nonsense. I'm not sure I believe it as fervently as she does, but there is something going on with her recipes I can't explain. Didn't the full-size Christmas tree growing out of the paper coffee cup convince you?"

Max shrugs.

"A clever trick, I'll admit," he says, "but it's not magic. There's no such thing."

Phaedre fills the greasy roasting pan with hot water and detergent and sets it aside. Filling one side of the sink with water and soap, she washes the bowls and dishes and silverware. There are no leftovers.

Phaedre hands the washed dishes over to Max who rinses them in the other side of the sink, stacking them in the drainer atop the counter in the tiny kitchen.

When they have finished, Max wraps his arms around

Phaedre's waist and kisses her neck. He makes it clear what he'd prefer to be doing. Phaedre reaches for the wrapped Christmas cookies on the dining table.

"I can't believe we're going through with this," Max tells her.

"Yes, we are, Max. And you're going to follow your grandma's instructions to the letter or you can forget about sex until next Christmas when you'll have another chance to redeem yourself. Do you want to open yours here or in the bedroom?"

"I'll stay here. You take the bedroom, Phaedre."

"All right. And no cheating. No peeking."

Phaedre and Max unwrap their custom gingerbread cookies from Mr. Hoffman. They smile at the same instant and have nearly the same thought.

That looks too much like Phaedre. I couldn't possibly bite into it.

That looks so much like Max. How could I possibly devour him?

But neither wishes to be the one to break the spell of Grandma's magic recipe.

Phaedre gnaws first at Max's feet, moving up to the knees and thighs, giving a little chuckle when she devours his privates. She saves the head for last. It is the part of the caricature in sugar frosting that most resembles him. She pops it in her mouth, but it is too big to swallow whole.

Closing her eyes, she bites down on Max's head, grinding it to bits. It is the sweetest part of the cookie with the most sugar frosting on it. She smiles to herself.

"There. I've done it. You're inside me now, Max. I've gobbled you up, my love."

She lays back on her pillow, looking up at the pattern of steam pipes and their shadows on the ceiling. She realizes she is horny and hopes Max hurries up with his cookie.

Max first bites off Phaedre's head, finding the cookie a bit too sweet. He manages to swallow her head whole. Now the cookie no longer resembles anyone, especially not someone he loves.

Max licks the cookie woman's breasts, her belly button,

and her vagina until all the frosting has melted into his mouth and only the gingerbread remains. Thinking of Phaedre, he nibbles the gingerbread until it is gone.

"Now you're part of me, my love. I've eaten you all up."

He thinks it was a pretty good cookie, possibly made with real ginger. He wonders if Phaedre has finished her cookie of him and knocks on the bedroom door.

"Are you finished with me, Phaedre?" he asks. "May I come in?"

She chuckles at his wordplay. "Please. I've been waiting for you."

Max finds her stripped naked, propped against many pillows, her legs in a pose he can only think of as seductive—except he's not thinking at all. His single-mindedness crowds out all thought.

Taking off his clothes while walking towards the bed, he gets tangled up and nearly topples on top of Phaedre.

"I'm glad you are so eager," she tells him. "Enthusiasm goes a long way with me."

His undershorts get snagged on his erection. Phaedre helps extricate him. They both laugh.

Phaedre and Max tell themselves they want to go slow so their love-making lasts, but they've been ready to jump on each other since their supper guests left. They were quite prepared to do it right on the dining room floor, the last course of their supper—dessert.

Phaedre straddles Max's stomach. She lowers herself slowly onto his erection, her breasts jiggling happily as she bounces up and down on her knees. They moan in unison.

The brevity of their love-making is outshone by its intensity. They collapse on their sides, theirs arms wrapped around each other, their legs entwined, breathing heavily.

"I've just had a crazy thought," Max says, propping himself up on one elbow. "I was just wondering. Will you marry me, Phaedre?"

"Oh, my God. Yes, Max. Of course I will marry you. I love you."

"I'm afraid I don't yet have an engagement ring, Phaedre. The idea to propose only just occurred to me."

"It's the sentiment that counts," she tells him.

"Oh, good. That's going to save me a lot of money."

She tickles his ribs. They lie down beside one another and get beneath the covers again.

"Max," she says. "I received this ring of polished amber from your grandmother yesterday, just in case you decided to pop the question."

"Just in case, huh?" he says.

"Well, she was right, wasn't she, Max? The ring belonged to your great-grandmother."

She places the small but heavy ring in his palm. It catches a glint from the bedside lamp.

Max takes up Phaedre's hand and places the ring on her finger. They smile and kiss each other with many long, slow kisses, only coming up now and then for air.

Phaedre admires the ring by the light of her bedside lamp. Then she turns the lamp down, and she and Max snuggle against each other. By the light of the streetlamps, they see it is snowing.

They spend the rest of Christmas telling each other the oldest and most outrageous stories they recall about their families. Now and then, Pharedre takes her hand from beneath the covers to look at her ring of amber.

It is the best Christmas either of them remembers.

———◦———

Fitz and Antonio rush inside their apartment across from Van Cortlandt Park in The Bronx. It was a cold and windy walk from the last stop on the 1 train at 242nd Street. They have only been sharing the one-bedroom apartment for a month.

They hold each other and kiss.

"That's the best way to warm up that I know of," Fitz tells his friend.

Antonio bends over to turn on the lights on their Christmas tree, the one grown from a seedling in a carry-out coffee cup. The little sprout was given to them by Madame Ana, their friend

Max's grandmother. Her instructions had been simply to give it a little water and to think good thoughts.

Fitz grabs Antonio's rear end as he fishes for something else beneath their tree.

"Careful," Antonio warns his buddy. "If you're naughty, Santa's not going to come."

"I'm not being naughty. I'm being nice. Besides, I think Santa's already been here."

Antonio stands up and hands Fitz a package wrapped in brown paper and tied with white string. They smile.

"Just a minute," Fitz says.

He retrieves a similarly wrapped package—also tied with white string—from beneath their bed. He hands the parcel to Antonio. They both laugh. Antonio unties the white string on his present.

"Maybe we should eat Madame Ana's Christmas cookies first," Fitz suggests. "Do you want to stay here in the living room or move to the bedroom?"

"I'll go in the bedroom," Antonio replies. "We'll open our other presents out here later, OK?"

"Sure," Fitz tells him. "I can't imagine what you've gotten me," he says, winking.

When Fitz hears Antonio close the bedroom door, he unwraps the cookie from its white paper. It is a sort of caricature, a cartoon version of Antonio rendered in frosting, wearing blue jeans, leather jacket, and biker boots. The face looks exactly like his buddy with its deep brown eyes and glistening black hair.

Fitz licks off Antonio's Levi's and boots, getting a little bit hard as he does so. He laps at the leather jacket until Antonio is naked, the hue of his skin the warm color of the gingerbread. Eating Antonio's brown cookie body, Fitz saves his head for last.

"Thank you, Madame Ana," he says. "Maybe it wasn't your intention, but that cookie has gotten me very randy."

In their bedroom, Antonio takes his cookie out of its paper. He laughs, thinking how much fun it will be to gobble his friend up. He breaks the gingerbread cookie in half and bites off Fitz's head. Then he devours his leather jacket. The frosting is too sweet but the cookie is good.

Antonio finishes eating Fitz's leather jacket and starts chewing on his boots and Levi's. He finds himself getting aroused.

"What a fun present," he says to himself. "Thank you, Madame Ana."

Antonio opens the bedroom door a crack and hollers out.

"Are you finished yet, buddy?" he asks.

"Yeah, I am," Fitz replies. "I've gobbled you all up."

Antonio joins Fitz in the living room. They sit on their slightly sagging secondhand sofa, admiring their Christmas tree. They hand each other their presents and kiss each other.

"Happy Christmas," Fitz tells his friend.

"Feliz Navidad," Antonio replies.

After removing the string and brown paper from their presents, they laugh heartily. As they suspected, they'd each gotten the other a pair of shrink-to-fit Levi's. The fact that they wear the same size only makes it more hilarious.

Antonio brings a bottle of tequila from the kitchen and two small glasses. Fitz retrieves his bottle of Old Curmudgeon whisky. They each enjoy one shot each of whisky and tequila. They feel quite feliz and happy.

Fitz places his hand on Antonio's thigh. Their blue jeans reveal growing boners.

"Want to break in our new Levi's?" Fitz suggests.

"Tonight?"

"Yeah, why not? It's still early," Fitz replies. "We're both plenty randy, thanks to those love-potion cookies."

"But how will we get dry?" Antonio asks.

"The landlord's pumping out plenty of heat tonight. We'll stay in the bathroom next to the riser pipes. We'll be dry in no time."

"OK, buddy," Antonio says. "It'll be fun. We haven't baptized new Levi's together in a while."

They lead each other by the hand to the bedroom where they strip down to their skin and put on their new, stiff, shrink-to-fit blue jeans.

Antonio and Fitz head to the bathroom. They close the

door and fill the old claw-foot tub with hot water. In no time, it feels like a sauna.

With Fitz at the front of the tub and Antonio sitting behind him, they slip down into the hot water, sucking in their breath. As the heavy denim begins to shrink on their bodies, the outline of their boners becomes clear. Antonio nudges closer to his partner and puts his arms around him. The water in the tub looks like a vat of bluing.

"Oh, this feels so good after our walk home in the cold," Fitz tells him.

"I hope it's going to feel even better," Antonio remarks as he strokes Fitz's boner through the crotch of his wet Levi's.

As Antonio rubs his own hard-on against Fitz's backside, they move closer to the edge of climax. Fitz makes deep purring noises. They try to slow down but are too eager.

Since Antonio is in charge of both their erections, it is not surprising that they cream their jeans at the same instant. He feels Fitz's throbbing boner as they both shudder. Antonio leans back in the tub and Fitz lies back against his chest. They shut their eyes and enjoy all the sensations their wet lovemaking has brought them.

When the water has grown merely warm, Fitz pulls out the stopper and drains the tub. The porcelain is stained blue by the indigo dye in their jeans.

They sit on the edge of the tub, Antonio at the back, Fitz in the front, letting most of the water and indigo drip from their Levi's and stream down the drain.

The two friends take turns either standing in front of the heat riser pipes or sitting opposite them on the lid of the commode, relishing the feeling of the denim shrinking up on their bodies.

They spend the rest of Christmas telling each other the oldest and most outrageous stories they recall about their families. It is the best Christmas either of them remembers.

I stand at the kitchen window watching curtains of snow

swirl around the towers of the George Washington Bridge. The rest of the family has gone to bed..

My daughter Moosha loved the ugly brocaded sofa cushions. Nina shrieked with delight over the polished amber bracelet. She loved it even more when she learned it had come from her great-grandparents.

I hope my simple recipes have brought happiness to the two young couples by helping them realize the depth of their love.

I brew a pot of tea and sit at the kitchen table. It is 11:30, only a half-hour of Christmas left to enjoy.

A rap at the kitchen window startles me. Nikolai has again climbed to our sixth-floor apartment via the fire escape.

My brother drives a rented limousine. He works on Christmas and other holidays to make extra money and earn generous tips.

Nikolai uses the fire escape because he does not like people in the hallways and on the elevator watching where he goes. No doubt it is a leftover fear from his years of being under the scrutiny of nosy neighbors back in Russia. They regularly reported his strange habits to the police as though strangeness were itself a crime.

"I am happy you made it, Nikolai," I tell him. "Merry Christmas."

"Merry Christmas, Ana," he says, kissing my cheeks. His cheeks are cold.

I pour hot tea into our glasses and add two sugar-cubes to each. I fetch the bottle of Lantern Fuel vodka from the pantry and pour two healthy splashes into our glasses.

"Za zdaróvye," we toast each other

My brother takes a thick envelope from his uniform jacket and hands it to me.

"I have given a little trinket to Nina that she will forget by next Christmas," he says. "But this is my overtime and tip money for her art school. She will be a great artist some day."

"Bless you, Nikolai. Moosha and I wondered how we could afford her art school. There is something that came for you, too," I tell him, withdrawing the envelope from our parents from my apron pocket and handing it to him.

He glances at it and then looks at me. I would not be surprised that he recognizes our mother's beautiful script, even after the passage of so many years. After breaking the seal, he opens the flap and takes out the letter. He unfolds it and takes his spectacles from his inside jacket pocket.

I watch my brother's face as he reads, noting the crisscross of lines and wrinkles, furrows and scars inscribed there. Two World Wars and the Revolution and the countless purges through which he passed have written their history on his flesh.

Nikolai re-folds the letter from our parents and places his hands over it. He trembles and shakes as though grappling with a powerful force. He stares at me, pleading in his sparkling blue eyes.

Tears well up. Only the dam of his will holds them back.

At last they burst forth, a tiny stream that becomes a torrent. His chest heaves and he leans forward, holding his head in his hands. Taking the handkerchief from his chauffeur's jacket, he sobs until my own heart is on the verge of breaking.

I get up and stand behind my brother, rubbing his shoulders and stroking his neck.

"Nikolai," I tell him. "Let it go. Let it all go."

His sobbing subsides. He dries his eyes and blows into his handkerchief. Sighing, he takes a few deep breaths and smiles up at me.

"I don't know whether your magic is anything more than trickery, my dear Ana. I have wanted to cry for over sixty years, but there were no tears left after our parents were arrested and taken away. Bless you, my sister. I have at last been washed and forgiven for all I have done."

I pour only a little vodka into our glasses and go back to my chair. Nikolai toasts to our health. He takes my hand and squeezes it.

"This is the best Christmas I remember, Ana. Not since I was twelve years old have I felt thrilled to be alive."

"Yes, me too, Nikolai. God has blessed us all with love and kindness."

His tears have refreshed my brother, washed him, made him as clean as the snow falling on the rungs and railings of the fire escape outside the kitchen window.

We tell each other our memories of the old family home in Odessa, shedding more tears, but also enjoying laughter until our sides ache.

Nikolai does not return to work this Christmas. There is enough money for Nina's art school. We talk at the kitchen table and drink tea—with just a little vodka—until the sun comes up and all the shadows melt away.

SANTA'S HELPERS

The dried leaves, wood shavings, and kindling at the bottom of the hearth catch quickly. The logs of piñon and aspen flare up, needing no persuasion from the bellows. Though there is not yet much heat emanating from the raised, hive-shaped fireplace, the warm glow is cheering. I feel better already.

Draping the bath towel over my head and shoulders, I lean forward to inhale the steam from the pot of hot water in which a good-sized lump of camphor has dissolved. I can almost smell it. I push my mug of ginger tea with peppercorns—a remedy of my mother's for head colds—closer to the fire, turning the handle towards me. This is not how I want to spend Christmas Eve nor, as my cold runs its course, how I care to spend the next few days.

In any house in which I've lived as an adult, it is my custom to build a raging fire in the fireplace on Christmas Eve. This year it seems doubly important because of my chills and fever. I push the pot of water closer to the glowing coals to encourage its boiling again. Sitting back in the wood rocker, I take another swallow of my spicy tea. In my state, it is utterly tasteless.

Comfortable at last, I doze for a time, recollecting the Christmas when I was seven years old and I learned there was no such person as Santa Claus. That day is not among my favorite memories. I recall it reluctantly. This Christmas Eve has not been much happier.

On that Christmas morning, now nearly forty years ago, I descended the steps from my small bedroom to the living room downstairs. I'd heard noises and hoped to catch Santa or one of his elves in the act of satisfying my every wish.

Making no noise in my Dr. Denton pajamas with feet, I came upon the scene of my parents munching on the sugar-sprinkled cookies and drinking the milk I had left for Santa the night before. I stood with my mouth open. I could not get any words out. I did not yet weigh enough to cause the stairs to creak. They hadn't heard me come down.

My father, wearing just his longjohns and a T-shirt, sat on the floor, several screwdrivers and wrenches arrayed around him in an arc. My mother consulted an enormous drawing, a schematic for assembling a tiny house, a dollhouse, no doubt for my sister Margaret. Pieces and panels of the doll's house were scattered all across the carpet, creating a strange geometric pattern. My mother sat on the footstool in her bathrobe.

"I know, dear," she said to my father, "but it clearly says to insert Tab A into Slot B. It may not make sense, but that's what the directions say to do."

My father pulled apart the pieces he had joined incorrectly and took another bite of Santa's Christmas cookie. My mother handed him a different section of the doll's house. They looked up and both spied me at the same time.

"Honey," my mother said. "What are you doing up? It's only..."

She glanced up at the clock on the mantle.

"Oh, dear," she remarked to my father. "It's 5:30 already. The sun will be up in an hour, and with it, I'm sure, little Margaret. I'm afraid we won't finish in time. Can you help us, Six?"

My sister was three years younger and a bit of a terror when she didn't get her way. I got my nickname from my great-grandfather, the original Sixtus Thorson.

"Where's Santa?" I asked them. "Why are you eating his cookies?"

"We got hungry, son," my father replied. "We've been at this since you and your sister went to bed last night."

"Did Santa leave anything for me?" I asked.

My parents looked quickly towards our Christmas tree. My mother tossed two pillows over the presents lying there. I got no more than a glimpse of the construction set I'd asked for.

"I'm afraid Santa didn't have time to wrap everything he brought you and Margaret. He got you both so much this year," my mother remarked.

"Why are you putting Margaret's dollhouse together, Dad?"

He fastened two sections of the ground floor of the two-storey dollhouse together and my mother handed him two more pieces.

"More people are born every year, Six," my father said, "but there's still only one Santa Claus. He can't keep up. So he assigns certain people, like your mother and me, to be his official helpers."

"He drops everything off to us and your father and I put things together, that's all," my mother said. "Can you help me find Section 12?"

I looked among the pieces of dollhouse scattered about, stepping carefully among them. It looked as though a tornado had burst through Tiny Town. I stole glimpses of what lay beneath the lowest branches of the tree. At last, I located Section 12.

"Give it to your father, Six," my mother said, checking the numbers on other parts.

"Did Santa even eat any of his cookies?" I asked, waiting to see who answered.

My parents glanced at each other.

"He said he was already quite full," my mother replied.

"He told us we could have them, son," my father said, "as a *Thank You* for helping him out."

"So how did Santa get in?" I asked. "You've got a fire going. How could he come down the chimbley?"

"That's *chimney*," my mama said. "There are other ways Santa can come in. Through the keyhole, for instance."

I handed my papa the screwdriver he was trying to reach.

"I think you are lying," I told them. "I think there's no such thing as Santa Claus. There never was. *You* are Santa Claus and I hate you both. Santa is a frog."

"I think you mean *fraud*, Six," my mother corrected. "F-R-A-U-D."

I stomped back up to my room, at least as far as stomping in padded footie pajamas was possible. Throwing myself onto the bed, I buried my face in the pillow and sobbed until I could hardly breathe. My father came into the room and sat down on my bed. I turned away.

"Please, Six," he told me, "don't carry on so. Don't waken your sister. Santa's helpers are not finished yet. Margaret's doll-house is proving more difficult than we imagined."

He rubbed my back and tousled my hair. It was no use. I hated him.

"I know how you feel, son. I'm sorry you had to find out in this way. It's nice to believe in Santa Claus as long as we can. Santa makes people feel good and he helps us do nice things for one another. Sometimes it's more fun to play Santa and bring joy to others than it is to receive his gifts. He doesn't have to be real to have a good effect on all of us, children and grown-ups alike."

"You tell me and Margaret to always be truthful, and then you tell us lies. I don't believe anything you and Mama tell me. You lied."

I turned my head away again and pushed my face into the pillow. My papa tried to tell me there are different sorts of lies, but I didn't care. They were all still lies. I clamped my hands over my ears until my father left the room.

Though I got my Erector Set and my sister got her lop-sided House Beautiful doll's house, Christmas was never the same. Though I'd been enlisted as another of Santa's helpers until Margaret came of age, I never enjoyed playing Santa as much as my mother and father did. While I forgave my parents for their well-meaning deception, I was never able to forgive Santa Claus himself for not actually being real. I hated him for it. And the roaring fire ensured he was never getting down *my* chimney.

Today began with a throbbing headache that intensified

when I sat up at the edge of the bed. I'd slept a lot longer than I'd intended. It was well after ten o'clock in the morning. My muscles and joints ached though I'd done no strenuous work since the beginning of the week.

Knowing the early signs of coming down with a bad cold or even the flu, I was happy to have the day off from Mila-Grow Nursery & Greenhouse. My seniority had counted for something. The nursery would be a madhouse with last-minute shoppers for balsam Christmas trees and wreaths. This was the day I'd set aside to decorate my own tree.

I got dressed slowly. Sudden moves made my head pound. I saw that my Levi's had developed a rip in one knee. My bootlace broke. I knotted the ends together and tied it as best I could.

Since my soon-to-be ex-wife, Benita, had decided to take all the Christmas decorations, I'd have to make a trip to the Lucky Happy Dollar Store to buy a new collection. I hated that place. It was always crowded with people who seemed to wander up and down the aisles trying to remember what they'd come for. I was one of them. I thought maybe I should also pick up some cough syrup.

My jacket was not on the hook behind the front door. I could not remember where I'd left it, and chose to leave home without it, wearing only my long-sleeve thermal undershirt.

Though the sun shone as brilliantly as a continuous camera flash, it was not warm out: probably still around freezing. I cranked the engine of my old turquoise pickup and turned the heater on full blast, hoping it would melt the frost on the windshield so I wouldn't have to get out to scrape it. It grew warm so gradually, I wasn't aware when it finally got warm. The rear window was still coated with frost on the inside. I couldn't quite see, so I sounded the horn before I backed up.

As I was about to turn onto the road, I saw my nineteen-year-old black cat, Irene, lying on her side in the driveway where she liked to sun herself for hours on end. Though I hadn't felt or heard anything, I realized I'd run over the poor creature because I was too lazy the clean the back window.

I flung the truck door open and jumped out. Kneeling

beside Irene, I pet her head and burst into tears. She'd been with me since my first year of college. *Why now?* I asked. *Why on Christmas Eve?*

Irene was already stiff. It was not that cold out, so she must have died in her favorite spot in her favorite posture and I simply rode over her corpse. I felt better that I hadn't killed her, but she was still dead. *Good night, Irene*, I sang in my head. *I'll see you in my dreams.*

I picked up my pet cat and moved her onto the door mat on the front porch. She seemed to be resting as though taking yet another nap. There was no blood because Irene was already frozen when I trampled her with my truck tires.

I'd left the door of my truck open. What little heat there had been escaped. I found my jacket behind the seat and put it on, but I was already chilled. The heater seemed to throw only cold air. I shivered. My cough grew more insistent. Though I hadn't left yet, I couldn't wait to get home.

The Lucky Happy Dollar Store was packed. The only boxes of Christmas tree ornaments remaining were all mismatched though equally ugly. There was not a single box left intact that didn't have at least three ornaments broken or missing. I didn't care. I bought four boxes and two strings of lights.

My next stop was the Red Willow Drug Store to get a bottle of cough syrup. The pharmacist recommended Haeck's Cough Remedy, a strange name, I thought, for those suffering from a hacking cough and congestion. The druggist recommended it over all other brands.

"Follow the instructions strictly," he cautioned. "Do not take too much. My customers tell me it's quite strong."

He also suggested dissolving camphor in hot water and inhaling the vapors. I had a recollection of my mother doing the same thing for me when I was a child. I thanked the pharmacist and paid for the cough syrup and the jar of camphor. He wished me a Merry Christmas. I slunk out, pretending I hadn't heard him.

It was snowing. Though it was only a light coating, it was quite slippery. I drove slowly and kept to the main road.

At the first and only stoplight on the way home, my brakes

did not stop me in time. My truck plowed into a wide-assed high-lifter pickup in front of me. I heard glass shatter and metal crumple. The other driver and I got out of our pickups simultaneously and inspected the damage.

"No harm done," the guy, somewhere in his twenties, said, adding, "Merry Christmas."

He got back in his truck as I stood in the road, other cars swerving around me.

I had no headlights or radiator grill, and both fenders had been crumpled in the accident. My bumper had not even been touched.

"No harm done?" I shouted. "What d'ya call this?"

But the other guy was long gone. I picked up what remained of the front grill and threw it in the back of my pickup. A car scooting around me nearly took my door off. The fellow did not wish me a Merry Christmas or anything close to it.

"Same to you," I hollered after him, holding up both center digits for emphasis.

I drove even slower the rest of the way home. My driveway was coated with ice, so I tread gingerly, hanging onto the rumpled fender of my truck until I could safely reach the bannister of the front porch. At least I hadn't dropped any of the Christmas ornaments or my cold remedies.

There sat Irene on the door mat, as flat a cat as I had ever seen. The ground was too frozen to be able to get a shovel into it. I'd have to store the unfortunate feline in my freezer until late March. I felt so bad losing her, even if I hadn't been responsible for her death.

Two letters had been stuffed into the mailbox beside the front door, one of them, a thick one, from my wife's attorney, Dewey, Cheatham & Howe. Though I knew the divorce papers were pending, *Couldn't it have waited until after Christmas?* I thought. I didn't need any more bad news today. I took my packages and letters inside, and set the ornaments and lights by the tree.

The other letter, from my employer, Mila-Grow Nursery & Greenhouse, contained a Christmas bonus check. *At last some good news.* But the letter in which the check had been wrapped informed me that Mila-Grow was closing for good on December 31st. I was now out of a job, too. *Thanks, Santa.*

I flung both the letter and the check at the Christmas tree and went into the kitchen. I was so chilled I kept my blanket-lined jean jacket on until I could light a fire.

Figuring my mother's tried-and-true cold remedy might also do me good, I prepared a mug of strong ginger tea into which I also dropped a few crushed peppercorns.

While my tea steeped, I fetched the bottle of Old Curmudgeon whisky from the cabinet above the fridge The brand had always been my Dad's favorite. Then I unscrewed the cap from the bottle of Haeck's Cold Remedy.

I poured a healthy dose of whisky into the tea and took a good swallow of the cough syrup. Maybe I should have bought two bottles of Haeck's. I went out back to the woodshed and hauled in more firewood, enough to last the night, to ensure that make-believe Santa Claus never got down my chimney.

The well-dried logs caught quickly. The fire was soon roaring. I fetched my mug of ginger tea and hung my jacket on the hook behind the front door. I was in for the night.

My head was too congested to taste the spicy tea. I opened the four partial boxes of ornaments, placing them on the sofa near the tree. I'd forgotten hooks, but I remembered my mother used paper clips for hooks when they'd run out. There was a brand new box of paper clips in the desk that had belonged to my grandfather.

I managed to get all the ornaments on the tree, breaking only one of them. As though I'd been sleepwalking, I barely remembered hanging a single one. My wife—my soon-to-be ex-wife—had always decorated our Christmas tree. This was my first time. The tree seemed crooked and uninspired.

Sitting down before the hearth, I finished my ginger tea. Though I felt a bit warmer, my cold felt as though it were getting worse. I ached all over and my head throbbed whether I was moving or sitting still. I went to the kitchen to make another tea.

This time I started with the Old Curmudgeon to make sure I was getting enough in my tea. I skipped the peppercorns since I could not taste them anyhow. Then I poured in a little more of the cough remedy. *It couldn't hurt,* I thought.

I went back to the living room with my mug of tea. There was no doubt my cold was making me woozy.

The short winter sun was already arcing towards the horizon. I realized I'd forgotten to hang the two strings of lights on the tree. They were at the bottom of the bag from the Lucky Happy Dollar Store.

Sipping my therapeutic tea as I worked hanging the lights on the tree, I managed only to knock a half-dozen more ornaments to the tile floor, every one of which smashed with a popping noise like the shattering of a light bulb. Maybe the lights were supposed to go on the tree first.

Letting the first string of lights dangle where they were, I gave up in frustration. I felt exhausted though I'd hardly done anything.

It was still early, but I went to the bedroom and got ready for bed, not sure when sleep would overtake me. I stripped out of my Levi's and workboots, keeping on my longjohns and thermal shirt and heavy socks. I slipped into my mocassins and draped an old Indian blanket, a family heirloom, over my shoulders.

I returned to the kitchen and put on a pot of water in which to melt the camphor. I lit the fire under the kettle to make more tea, into which I poured equal amounts of Old Curmudgeon and Haeck's Cough Remedy.

I gave the logs in the fireplace a poke and added another. My tea was hot and the pot of water with camphor was steaming. I moved it closer and inhaled the vapors beneath a towel over my head. I was happy for the raised hearth, glad I didn't have to bend over to feed the fire.

I had no doubt this had been one of the worst days I'd had in long while. It was possibly the worst Christmas Eve in memory. I waited only for drowsiness to overtake me and make the rest of the evening vanish in the fog of sleep.

I moved over to the sofa so I wouldn't tumble out of the chair and land in the fireplace. *Except for bad luck,* I thought, *I wouldn't have had any luck at all today.*

The sound of scratching at the front door slowly creeps into my consciousness and at last jars me awake. I realize I hadn't put poor Irene in a plastic bag and moved her to the freezer to await burial beneath her favorite tree in the spring. The coyotes are probably making a fine meal of my unfortunate pet.

It is dark enough now that I need to switch on a light. The string of tiny lights dangling from the Christmas tree have not been plugged in. I get up from the sofa that seems to want to engulf me. My joints are stiff and creaky.

Switching on the outside light by the front door, I see that Irene still lies unmolested on the doormat. Flecks of snow speckle her black fur. It is too dark to see anything beyond my front porch. I pull Irene and the doormat inside. I think of making another tea with a splash of Old Curmudgeon. It is time I have another dose of Haeck's Cough Remedy, too.

When I turn around to go back into the living room, I see a huge fellow standing beside the fireplace. Though I hadn't fed the fire since I fell asleep, it is roaring. The man is dressed like a traditional Santa Claus in a red suit with furry white trim. His beard looks authentic, though until I can pull on it, I assume it is fake, like everything about Santa.

"Ho, ho, ho," he bellows from way down in his belly.

"Ha, ha, ha," I reply. "I don't believe in you. You're the result of whisky and cough syrup."

I would have armed myself with the poker except that the large man stands between me and the fireplace tools. I can't think how he got in. I lunge for the poker, the Indian blanket falling from my shoulders.

Suddenly, Santa is behind me. In the crook of his arm is a black kitten whose eyes follow me.

"Merry Christmas, Six," Santa tells me.

"You know who I am?" I ask.

"I know who everyone is, young man. Have my helpers arrived yet?"

"And who might they be?"

"Your parents, Six. Don't you remember?"

"My parents are both dead."

"Yes, that's true. Nevertheless..."

The burly fellow pretending to be Santa Claus sets the kitten on the floor. She heads directly for me and rubs her sides against my shins, her tail held high. Looking up at me with her huge eyes, she mewls.

"Helen is probably hungry. Mrs. Claus had her hands full with all the new pets."

"Helen, huh?" I remark.

Smelling the milk first to make sure it hasn't curdled, I pour some into a small bowl and set it on the floor. Filling the teakettle, I put it on the burner and retrieve the bottle of Old Curmudgeon.

The whiskers of the fellow playing Santa appear genuine: they are not pure white like artificial Santa beards. There's a bit of gray mixed in.

He seems amiable enough and I ask if he'd care for some milk and cookies.

"I am absolutely stuffed to the gills with milk and cookies, young man, but I wouldn't mind a wee dram of yon Old Curmudgeon."

"Don't you have other stops tonight?" I chuckle. "I wouldn't want to be responsible for your getting in an accident and disappointing millions of kiddies when you fail to deliver their hearts' desires."

"That's very considerate of you, Six, but my reindeer know the ropes. The sleigh practically drives itself. Thanks to my many helpers, I'm a bit ahead of schedule tonight."

"I see," I say, pouring a little bit of whisky into a teacup and handing it to him.

I decide to forego my tea and pour whisky into my cup, too, raising it to the make-believe Santa Claus.

"Skoal," he says, tapping my teacup with his.

"Salud," I tell him. "That means *Health*."

"Yes, I know," he says. "I understand all languages."

"Of course you do," I reply.

The raspy doorbell rings. The Santa stand-in swallows the last of his whisky and puts his cup in the sink.

"That must be my helpers. Thank you for the spot of Christmas cheer, Six. God be with you."

I follow the man in the fur-trimmed red suit to the front door. He opens it and lets out another trademarked *Ho-ho-ho.*

"Mom. Dad," I say. "What're you doing here? You're dead."

"Well, it's nice to see you, too, son," my dad says, laughing.

"Perhaps we are dead, Six," my mother adds. "But, here we are. Merry Christmas."

My imaginary Santa steps onto the porch where he has left his sleigh whip leaning against the railing. He waves good-bye with his huge red mitten. My parents step into the living room and I shut the door. I suspect their appearance is also the result of mixing Old Curmudgeon whisky with Haeck's Cough Remedy. They are dressed in red and green like Christmas elves.

My mother and father both hug me; my mother kisses me. But I do not feel anything. They are like faint breezes on my skin. They are not quite a hundred percent. They are slightly see-through. My new kitten rubs herself against them. They must be at least partly present.

"There you are, sweet Helen," my mother says to the kitten, picking her up and cradling her, petting her tummy.

"How did she come by the name Helen?" I ask. "That's kind of an unusual name for a cat."

"*Betty* was already taken," my father says.

"Mrs. Claus names new pets after famous people," my mother explains. "She was named for Madame Helena Blavatsky."

"Who?" I ask.

"It's not important," my father remarks. "Helen is yours now. You can give her another name if you like. What have you to drink, son?"

"Whisky," I reply. "Your favorite, Dad: Old Curmudgeon."

"No eggnog?" my mother asks. "It's that season of the year."

"No," I say. "I haven't been feeling too good, Mom. I should get back to bed."

"Let us enjoy our visit, Six. Aren't you happy to see us?"

"Yes, of course, but..."

"But what?"

"You're probably not real. I'm hallucinating or something. I'm just lonely, that's all."

"Is that what you think?" my dad asks. "Then how do you explain Helen, the cat?"

"Look, Dad. If I can hallucinate you and Mom, it'd be a breeze to hallucinate a little cat, don't you think?"

"Why would you want to, Six?" he asks. "An imaginary cat is not going to curl up at the foot of the bed and keep your feet warm."

"If you have the ingredients, Six," my mom says, "I can whip up a batch of eggnog for us."

I lead them into the kitchen. My mother rummages through the refrigerator. She asks for a mixing bowl and a whisk. My father points to the bottle of whisky. I take down three glasses.

My mother has the eggnog whipped up in no time. She fills the three glasses using the soup ladle. My father pours a healthy dose of whisky into each glass.

"Go easy, George," my mother cautions.

"Why?" he asks. "It's not like I have to drive. We can float home."

We take our glasses to the living room. My mother carries the bowl of eggnog and my father the bottle of Old Curmudgeon. My parents and I toast one other.

"You need to add nutmeg to your grocery list, son," my mother suggests. "And what's the story with your bedraggled Christmas tree, Six? It's dreadful."

"I got sick, Mom. I never finished decorating it. It's hard to get in the spirit when you're not feeling good."

"Well, we're here to help, darling. We're Santa's helpers, remember? George, you string the lights on the tree. You were always so good at that: always balanced, no dim spots. I'll hang the ornaments."

Real or not, Mom has taken over. My father puts the lights on the tree in under a minute. My mother has the surviving ornaments on the branches in less time than that. The are no bare spots. The Christmas tree looks as good as any I remember growing up: good enough to adorn a shop window.

"Thank you, Mom, Dad. I'm afraid I was not up to the job."

"You're welcome, son," my father says. "What about your poor old cat, Irene? Do you want help with her?"

"The ground will stay frozen until spring, Dad. Can you help me stuff her in the freezer?"

"Not where you have food," my mother complains. "It's not sanitary."

"Irene was clean," I remind her.

"Where's your shovel?" my father asks.

"It's out back in the shed. But you're not going to get a shovel in the ground. It's as hard as concrete."

"I'll just heat up the blade of the shovel. I'll get her little grave dug. Got a match?"

"Sure, Dad. I got a whole box of 'em," I say, taking the box of matches from beside the hearth. "But you're not going to get a shovel hot with matches."

"Where would you like Irene buried, son?"

"Her favorite spot was in the old cottonwood grove."

"Lots of winding roots," my father remarks, "but I'll get her planted. Don't you worry."

My father dons his red Santa's helper cap and goes out to the kitchen. I hear him close the back door. My mother and I sit on the sofa facing the fire.

"We'll have a little nightcap when you father gets back," she tells me. "You really should trust you father, Six. He always gets the job done."

"I suppose," I reply. "But I'm a landscaper, Ma. I know how the ground gets in winter. And this year we had a lot of rain in November. It's frozen solid."

"How do you like your job, Six? Do you still find it fulfilling?"

"Yes, I do—or, rather, I did. I'm afraid the owner has sold the business. I'm out of work."

"We heard that might happen," my mother tells me. "I

hope you don't mind. We sent your application to the new owner. He is only too happy to have you on board, with your experience and all. You should be receiving your letter of hire any day now."

The kitchen door bangs open. My father enters. His cheeks are rosy like a true Santa's helper. The fire flares in the hearth from the burst of air. I add another log. My mother goes into the kitchen.

"Irene seems quite content, my boy," my Dad tells me. "There's a little space between the roots if you'd like to add a small marker—a couple of stones maybe."

"Thanks, Dad. I'm surprised you got it accomplished."

He smiles with a wide grin, a lot more expressive than he used to be. My mother returns with three glasses of eggnog on a tray. She does not remind me again about nutmeg. They sit down on either side of me on the sofa.

"To your health, Six," my parents toast.

"And to yours as well," I say.

"Too late for that," my father says. Turning to my mother, he asks, "Martha, did you tell him about Victoria at the bank?"

"No, not yet, dear. I was waiting for you. Let's tell him now."

"Well, Six," my father says, hanging his head a little sheepishly. "Your mother and I also wanted to help you out in the romance department."

"We didn't want you to feel bad after your divorce from Benita."

"What did you do?" I ask.

"Nothing that wasn't headed in that direction anyhow, Six," my father says. "We just gave it a little more gas."

"We know Victoria is crazy about you, Six."

"What? Do you snoop on people from up there—or wherever you came from."

"*Out there* might be a better way to phrase it," my father says.

"It's not snooping exactly," my mother explains. "It's not like we peer into people's minds or anything. All we can do is watch."

"Thank God," I say. "So what did you see?"

"Victoria sat at her desk in idle moments sketching your

likeness—over and over. She's a very good artist, quite competent."

"Really," I say.

A little embarrassed, I get up to tend the fire. I like Victoria a lot, too. I'm a little bit surprised she noticed me.

I return to the sofa. My mother has refilled our eggnog. I can definitely taste a good dose of Old Curmudgeon in it. My parents look a bit more substantial now, or else my vision has gotten blurry.

"Then, at the bottom of one of the sketches," my mother goes on, "she signed her name and yours, *Victoria Thorson.*"

"Really?" I ask.

"Yes," my father says. "So we sent her a dozen roses—in your name, of course. You know, your handwriting is a lot like mine."

"Where'd you get the money? I thought no one has money up there."

"Don't believe everything you hear," my father cautions. "The world is nothing like you read about."

"I suppose we should be going, Six," my mother says. "I've made you another ginger and peppercorn tea. It's steeping on the stove."

"Add a splash or two of Old Curmudgeon for me," my father says, raising his glass of eggnog and downing the last of it. "If there's nothing else you need, son, your mother and I will be on our way."

"Oh, there is," I tell him. "I had a little fender bender this afternoon and I was wondering... you know."

"Oh, that," my mother remarks. "We took care of that on the way in."

"Good as new," my father adds.

My parents put on their Santa stocking caps. They enfold me in their arms and spin me around until I am dizzy. I close my eyes.

"Not so fast, George," my mother warns. "He's woozy."

"Merry Christmas, son," they both tell me.

"And to all a good night," my dad says.

Though the front door neither opens nor closes, my parents leave. Owing to the many strange events the evening held for me, I'm prepared to believe they disappeared through the keyhole.

The clock says it is 11:30. I guess I'd fallen asleep. The fire is nearly out, but the hearth is still putting out heat. My head feels less congested and my cough has vanished. My vision, though, is still a little blurry.

The new cat, at least, is apparently real, though I'm not sure about any of the rest of it. Helen lies curled up in my lap, purring gently. The decorated Christmas tree and the three empty glasses of eggnog appear real enough, too—at least for now.

I am exhausted and head to the bedroom. Little Helen weaves in and out between my feet and follows me, mewing when we pass her empty saucer in the kitchen. I pour in some more milk.

Crawling into bed in my longjohns and thermal shirt and thick socks, I switch off the light. I am nearly asleep when I feel the bounce of Helen jumping up onto the bed. She circles a couple of times before settling down, nudging up against my feet. It is enough to make *me* want to purr.

My father had told me, "An imaginary cat is not going to curl up at the foot of the bed and keep your feet warm."

I suppose he is right.

Somehow, it has turned out to be the best Christmas Eve I remember.

ORPHANS IN THE STORM

The Ornery Burro is closing at eight tonight, just a half-hour to go. Two couples at the front of the bar get up, saying goodnight to Lloyd, the bartender. They all are dressed up, though the women outshine the men. They look like they might be going to a Christmas Eve party. They are a jolly bunch. I smile at them.

Their departure leaves only me and one other guy who sits at the far end of the bar. I turn to look at him. We met a few times. His name comes easily to mind.

"Antonio," I exclaim. "I'm sorry. I didn't know that was you sitting back there. Feliz Navidad," I tell him, raising my bottle of Dos Equis. He is drinking the same.

"Happy Christmas," he replies, coming over to occupy the stool next to me. "Looks like we'll be closing this place up."

"Looks that way," I say. I extend my hand and he shakes it.

"Your name is Sixtus, right?"

"Yeah, but nobody actually calls me that. Everybody calls me *Six*. What about you? Do you go by *Tony*?"

"No. I like my full name: Antonio."

"I thought you'd be with your girlfriend tonight for sure," I tell him.

"Girlfriend?" he asks.

"The Mexican stunner with the deep brown eyes," I reply. "I've seen you two together a couple times. She seems to like wearing red and it likes her, too. "

Antonio looks puzzled for a few seconds and then smiles.

"She's my cousin, Alicia. We pal around sometimes. She's the only member of my family who will have anything to do with me."

"That's unfortunate, especially at Christmas. I can't imagine why."

"A long story, I'm afraid, Six. It makes me feel like an orphan at times. Where is your family? I'm surprised you're not with *them* tonight."

"Most of my family are back East. Some are even further back than that—in Norway. I guess we're both orphans this Christmas."

We swallow the rest of our beers and wish the bartender a Merry Christmas. Antonio and I fetch our jackets from the row of hooks by the entrance. I wear a worn leather biker jacket—though I've never ridden a motorcycle. Antonio wears a blanket-lined denim jacket and a black felt cowboy hat. We stand outside beneath the small awning overhanging the front door, surprised by the swirling snow.

"Care to look for another joint that's open?" I suggest. "I mean, since neither of us has any place to be tonight."

I don't want it to seem like I'm coming on to him since I'm pretty sure Antonio likes women. I'd just like not to have to spend Christmas Eve alone. Maybe he feels the same.

"We're not going to find any place open tonight, Six, especially with the bad weather," Antonio says. "Tell you what: Why don't you come over to my place? It's not far, just a little ways out on the mesa. We'll have our nightcap there."

"Fine," I tell him. "Just a nightcap, though. I'll follow you."

"Great," Antonio says. "I'll be glad to have some company on Christmas Eve."

We turn our collars up to the wind and snow. Antonio pulls the wide brim of his cowboy hat down. We head to our pickup trucks in the gravel lot out front of The Ornery Burro. Neither of our trucks is anywhere close to new. My old Ford is twenty years old, from the '50s. Antonio's pickup is a blue Chevy of only slightly newer vintage.

I climb into my old turquoise pickup, brushing the inch of snow off my windshield using the wipers. I follow Antonio's taillights out to where the night is utterly black and the snow in the headlights is a blinding swirl. His red taillights become hard to make out at times. My squeaky wipers have a tough time keeping up with the pelting snow.

Antonio slows down and enters a rutted road, pulling into the yard beside an adobe *casita* with a stand of *piñon* on either side. The snow has abated, but the wind is still whipped up. We hurry inside, stomping our boots on the door mat. Following his example, I hang my biker jacket on a peg on the back of the front door. Antonio switches on a lamp.

His house is quite tiny, but well-designed, featuring walls of white adobe plaster, *tierra blanca*, ceiling *vigas* and *latillas*, and a beehive-shaped fireplace in the corner of the living room.

"Welcome to my home, Six," Antonio tells me. "My *abuela* left me this place—going on five years ago now. She knew how much I loved spending time with her here. We talked for hours. It's been my home since the summer I finished high school and moved out of my parents' house."

"It's a cozy little place," I tell him, "especially on such a stormy night."

"It's all I need, really, though if I met someone and settled down, I might want to add another room."

He moves aside the fireplace screen, stirs the embers, and sets three logs standing upright at the back of the conical hearth. They catch almost at once, sending their light and warmth into the parlor. There are portraits of stiffly-starched ancestors on either side of the fireplace. The leaded-glass lamps on the two end tables look very old and fragile. The bookshelf against the wall is loaded to sagging.

Passing the small bedroom, I follow Antonio into the kitchen. In one corner, behind a curtain that's been drawn aside, sits an old claw-foot porcelain tub and a toilet. On the opposite side of the kitchen sink drainboard is a hand pump for water. Heat still emanates from the wood stove. He pokes the coals and adds a log.

Antonio takes two small glasses from the cupboard and brings out a bottle of tequila and an unopened bottle of Old Curmudgeon whisky.

"The whisky's from an old buddy. My drink is tequila. Take your pick, Six."

"Well, when in Rome," I tell him. "Tequila is good."

He carries the nearly-full bottle of tequila and the glasses back to the living room, setting them down on a long coffee table made from weathered planks. We sit down on the slightly lumpy settee and Antonio pours some tequila in each of our glasses.

"*Salud*," he toasts, raising his glass. "Merry Christmas, Six."

"My family says *God Jul*," I tell him, clinking his glass with mine, and taking a sip.

He smiles, repeating my Norwegian toast.

Antonio gets up and goes to the corner of the living room opposite the fireplace where there is a small Christmas tree on a table. I hadn't noticed it. As he bends over to plug in its string of multicolored lights, I see how nicely his Levi's fit him. I imagine holding Antonio, just holding him, in front of the fire. Sighing, I tell myself it's OK to make a warm wish on a cold Christmas.

The tree is decorated in a manner good enough to adorn a shop window. All the ornaments appear handmade, fashioned out of wood and tin, yarn and corn husks and colored beads. There's a carved nativity scene beneath the lowest branches. I get up to have a closer look at the crèche and Antonio returns to the settee.

The figures of the Holy Family, the sheep and shepherds and cattle, and the Magi upon their camels are quite marvelous. While nearly abstract in their simplicity, it is clear from a few details who each of the figures represents. The Wise Men are at the back of the table, nearly hidden by the lowest pine branches, as if to say they are on their way but have not yet reached the stable in Bethlehem. The clothing of all the statues is rendered with just a few shallow cuts and streaks of color.

"I really like your little tree, Antonio," I tell him. "Did you decorate it yourself?"

"I did," he says, smiling. "I always had a hand in decorating my family's tree."

I sit down beside him again on the tiny sofa. Antonio's handsomeness is striking, augmented by his longish raven-black hair and bottomless brown eyes. I am nearly his opposite, fair and blue-eyed. My heart thumps when I look at him. I wonder if he can hear it?

"I don't want to push you past your limit, Six," he says. "Care for a little more?"

"All right. Just a little. That'll be my nightcap."

The amount he pours is a little less than I would have liked. He seems to sense it and tilts the bottle again, flashing another of his smiles. I think I'd better get myself home before I start really falling for him. It is never a good idea to fall for a straight man.

"I want to ask you about your crèche, Antonio. Has it been in your family for a long time? Did someone you know carve it ? I'd love to learn woodcarving some day."

"I carved them, actually—a few years back, when I was still in high school. I'm a carpenter and cabinetmaker. I could loan you my old set of chisels and help you out with a couple pointers, if you'd like."

"Sure, Antonio. I'd love you to show me how. This year I never even put up a tree."

"Why not?"

"Not in the right mood, I guess. It's tough spending holidays alone," I tell him.

"Yeah, I know about that."

"But why you?" I ask. "You could have any woman you want, maybe even two or three."

He smiles, and splashes some tequila in his glass. He offers the bottle to me and I shake my head. He takes a healthy swallow from his glass before answering my question.

"I'm sorry, Six. I hope I don't frighten you off. I've had a pleasant time with you tonight. But I'm not interested in women. I like men."

My heart nearly leaps out of my chest. Certain shock has registered on my face, I search for something to say. Nothing comes out.

"That's also why my family, all strict Catholics, have disowned me. My cousin Alicia is the only one who speaks to me. The only other person who accepted me as I am was my grandma. Since she died, I've gotten used to spending holidays alone. I miss her a lot."

"Jeeze, man. I'm so sorry. I had no idea. I took you for absolutely straight."

As much as I want to, I can't bring myself to tell Antonio I like men, too. I have never told anyone, barely even myself. My heart beats like a drum.

I finish my glass of tequila and stand up, fetching my jacket from the back of the door. My hands tremble. I want to stay so bad, but I'm afraid what might happen if I do.

"I'm sorry, Six. Now I've scared you off. That wasn't my intention at all. I was just trying to level with you."

"You didn't scare me off, Antonio. It's ten o'clock. I've got to be going."

Antonio opens the front door. A blast of wind flings the door wide open, nearly knocking us both off our feet. Swirls of snow force their way inside. He pushes his shoulder against the door in order to close it. There is a drift of snow inside the door at our feet.

"It doesn't look like a good night for travel," Antonio says. "I think you'd better figure on spending the night, Six. I wouldn't want you to take a chance trying to make it home."

We face each other by the front door. Standing in my own fantasy, I cannot move. My heart pounds so loudly I cannot hear anything else.

Antonio helps me off with my leather jacket and hangs it back on the hook. Putting his hand on my shoulder, he leads me back into the living room.

"I'll curl up on the loveseat tonight," he tells me. "You can take the bed."

"Are you turning in now, Antonio? I don't want to keep you up."

"No, I'll be staying up for Christmas. I usually go to midnight mass, but not on a night like this. God understands. He's the One making it snow."

Antonio tugs his flannel shirt back on over his thermal shirt. He stirs the fire before placing another log on it. We sit down on the settee and he pours himself a small drink.

"You still go to church even though..." I ask him, not knowing how I should finish my thought.

"Yeah, even though the Church has no use for me, I still believe in God. Besides, Jesus doesn't turn anyone away, least of all a sinner like me."

"You have a generous heart," I tell him.

"I try to be kind," he says, modestly, "and often fail. Would you care for another shot of tequila?"

"Yeah, sure," I tell him. "I guess I'm not driving anywhere tonight, especially with my tires almost bald."

We raise our glasses and toast one another.

"I'll make a light supper later. If you're hungry, you're welcome to join me, Six. My larder's full. We could survive here until spring."

Fidgety, I get up and approach Antonio's Christmas tree and crèche. I ask whether I may examine one of the carved figures. My eye is drawn particularly to the Virgin. The angles and curves and shadows, and her spare expression, are especially striking. Antonio has liberated the figure from the knotty piñon rather than imposing the Virgin's shape upon the wood.

"That's my favorite figure, too. I'm happy you are drawn to it."

I replace the wooden statue and return to the settee, squirming in my seat. Antonio senses my unease.

"I'm afraid my coming out to you has made you uncomfortable, Six. I'm really sorry," he says. "I want you to like me, to be my friend, that's all. You can't keep things from your friends. I'll go sit in the rocker. I want you to be comfortable in my house."

"No, please. Stay here, Antonio. I think I'm the one making us both ill at ease. I haven't been exactly honest with you."

"How so?"

"I'm alone tonight—well, I *was* alone tonight—because I'm hardly the ladies' man you think, Antonio. I like men, too," I say. "I like you, in fact—since the first time I laid eyes on you."

I'm sure I am bright red. I want to look away, to turn my gaze from him, but I cannot. I peer directly into the deep wells of his eyes.

Watching his expression to make sure I'm not out of bounds, I rest my hand lightly on his thigh. I feel his heat through his Levi's. We lean towards one another, as though about to kiss, but we do not.

"I don't know whether you believe in prayer, Six. I struggle with my faith, like passing in and out of rain clouds on a long stretch of highway. Mostly, it is raining."

I smile. He squeezes my hand and goes on.

"I'm damn lonely out here, Six. I pray for someone to love, to be my new best friend like I had when I was ten years old—but with the grown-up stuff added. I wonder if it's the right kind of prayer."

"How could God be against love, Antonio? There'd be nothing for the devil to do."

He laughs. I notice his sly dimples.

"I'd like to be your friend, too, Antonio," I tell him. "We can work on the *best* part a little at a time, I guess."

"I'd like that," he says.

Antonio picks up the tequila bottle and our empty glasses. I follow him into the kitchen. He rinses the glasses, sets them upside down on the drainboard, and puts the bottle of tequila back in the cupboard. He pumps a pot full of water and places it on the woodstove. It sputters and sizzles.

"I'm afraid my family's custom for Christmas Eve supper is kind of spare," he tells me. "We'll have some smoked salmon with rice and beans. My family also ate apple slices, walnuts, and cloves of garlic dipped in honey before our meal."

"Jeeze, Antonio. That's pretty remarkable. My family had *lutefisk*, a kind of pickled fish we ate with plain boiled potatoes at Christmas. On the side, we had apples, prunes, and garlic dipped in honey."

"Yeah, that is pretty extraordinary," he says. "Our ancestors lived on nearly opposite sides of the globe, but we share certain Christmas customs. This night has been full of coincidences and surprises, don't you think?"

"If I didn't know better, Antonio, I'd think someone arranged our getting together tonight," I tell him.

He smiles. Facing him, I place both hands on his shoulders. He wraps his arms around my waist and draws me nearer. I rest my forearms on his shoulders. We are close enough to kiss. This time we do so—slowly. I feel as though my heart is going to burst forth from my chest.

"Whoa," I tell him. "I'm gonna have a heart attack."

"Not on my account, buddy," he says. "Let's go slow then. There's no hurry. Getting to know someone takes time. And it should be fun, don't you think?"

"I do," I say. "I tend to be too serious. You'll have to tell me when I need to lighten up."

"Sure. As long as you do the same for me."

As Antonio prepares the rice and fish, I take the paring knife, peeling and slicing an apple. I crack open several walnuts and extract the meat. Then I break off a few garlic cloves and strip off their husks. We glance back and forth at each other, smiling when we catch the other looking.

We decide a single bottle of beer between us will be enough with our supper. Antonio sets the simple table and puts out the rice and beans and smoked fish.

"Will you say our grace, Six?" he asks, lighting the single candle on the table.

"Me?"

Antonio nods and lowers his eyes. I feel unworthy of the honor. I have to wing it.

"Dear Lord, thank you for the food that is set before us. Thank you, too, for the lesson of kindness, shining above us like the star that guided the Wise Men. Bless me and Antonio, and bless our new friendship. Amen."

Antonio takes a deep breath and exhales. Smiling, he opens his eyes.

"Thank you, Six. That was an awfully good prayer for such an ordinary meal."

We take our seats. We dip the fruit and nuts and garlic

in the pot of honey. Antonio puts one of the apple slices in my mouth. I lick his fingers. When we have polished off the "appetizers," we begin on the rice and beans and smoked salmon. The tequila has given me an appetite.

We laugh a lot. Our conversation is easy, our questions gentle. I am falling for Antonio in a way that has nothing to do with my intense physical attraction to him. Put simply, I like him. I want to be his friend..

"Maybe it is God who brings people together," Antonio suggests, "but it is we who have to do the work. I am looking forward to getting to know you, Six. We cannot ignore the Almighty's invitation, can we?"

"No, I suppose not. I expect I'll enjoy getting to know you too, buddy."

We clear the table. There are no leftovers. Antonio pulls aside the kitchen window curtain. It is still howling outside. He pumps water into the sink and adds hot water from the stove. Antonio washes and I dry.

When the dishes are done, Antonio comes up behind me, putting his arms around me and giving my neck a peck. The sensation gives me a shiver and an immediate boner. He leaves an arm draped over my shoulder and we go back into the living room. The fire is putting out plenty of heat—almost as much as Antonio and I. We sit down on the small sofa.

Antonio leans back against the upholstered armrest and draws me to him. I lie back against his chest. I get in synch with the rhythm of his breathing and listen to his heartbeat. I tilt my head and look up at him.

"At the rate the snow is piling up tonight, Six, maybe God intends for us to spend a couple of days together getting to know each other. My road never gets plowed."

"It'll be OK," I tell him. "This is our slowest season at Mila-Grow Nursery & Greenhouse. That's where I work. After the Christmas trees and wreaths, there's nothing much doing until spring clean-up."

"*That's* where I've seen you. You caught my eye, too, let me tell you. I guess you grow the trees and I chop them up," he says, chuckling. His chest rocks up and down.

"I'd hardly call your carvings *chopping*, Antonio. They're beautiful. I haven't seen a style like yours before, either. It's old-fashioned and modern at the same time."

The wall clock chimes midnight. We sit up on the settee. Antonio leans towards me and kisses me. I kiss him back.

"Feliz Navidad," I tell him

"God Jul," he replies..

Antonio asks whether I'd like one more drink before turning in. I say I wouldn't mind. He returns from the kitchen with the bottle of Old Curmudgeon whisky and two short glasses.

"That's my favorite brand," I tell him. "But it's way too expensive for me."

"I couldn't afford it, either. I am rich in many things, Six, but money isn't one of them."

We laugh. He uncorks the wax-sealed bottle and pours us each a healthy dose.

"You drank my tequila, so it's only fair I try some whisky. It's courtesy of an ex-boyfriend."

We touch our glasses and wish each other good health. It is the kind of whisky one sips.

"So what's your experience with men so far?" Antonio asks. "Thumbs up or down?"

I nearly swallow wrong.

"I have zero experience with men, Antonio. I had a friend in early high school and we kissed and got each other off a couple times. But that's it. There's been no one since. He's married now and I'm lonely."

"I hear you, Six," he says, touching my cheek with his palm. "There's not many chances for men who like men to meet in these parts. I've had exactly that one boyfriend in the five years since I graduated high school. We lasted for two months. I liked his Levi's and leather jacket, but I didn't care much for the guy inside the clothes."

I smile and nod my head. We sip the last of our whisky.

"What do you say? Should we turn in, Six?"

"Yeah, I'm pretty beat and it's late."

"Then you take my bed. I'll curl up out here. My grandma left me plenty of blankets and quilts."

"No, I don't want to kick you out of your own bed, Antonio."

"Sorry," he says. "I'm sleeping out here. You're the guest."

We get up from the loveseat. Antonio turns out the Christmas tree lights and pokes at the fireplace embers before putting on two final logs. We go into the kitchen, where he puts the whisky bottle back in the cupboard and the glasses in the sink, filling them with water from the pump.

Going to the window, we stand looking out to the back yard, our noses up to the cold panes. It is difficult to tell how hard it is snowing. The wind seems to be coming from every direction in a whirlwind. Snow blows down from the roof and flies up from the ground. Our pickup trucks are shapeless mounds.

Antonio reaches behind me and slides his left hand into the left pocket of my Levi's. I do the same on his right side, enjoying yet another new sensation, a thrilling familiarity with another man. Antonio switches off the yard light and draws the curtain.

"Aren't you glad you decided to stay, Six?"

"I sure am. For a couple of reasons," I tell him. "First off, I don't think I would have made it home. And it's nice to be with someone on Christmas—to be with you, Antonio."

He shows me to the bedroom and turns on the lamp on the bedside table. It is a small room with a chest of drawers and a large armoire in the corner. The bed has an old-fashioned lacquered brass bedstead. The single window is completely frosted over with ghostly ferns. Though it is next to the living room and the fireplace, the room is cold.

"Good night, Six," he says, kissing my cheek. "You know where to find me if there's anything you need. Sleep tight."

"You, too, Antonio. Thank you for putting me up tonight."

Antonio lights an old kerosene railroad lantern atop the dresser and switches off the bedside lamp.

"Just in case you have to get up during the night," he explains, and goes out.

The lantern casts a cheerful glow around the room. I feel cared for, like when I was a kid.

I undress quickly, putting my boots at the foot of the bed, and stripping out of my Levi's. I keep my longjohns and T-shirt and wool socks on and crawl between the freezing sheets. The bed is a little lumpy, but there are plenty of covers. I warm up in no time.

Three times I am nearly asleep when I hear a groan from the parlor, accompanied by creaking from the old loveseat. I crawl out from under the covers and make my way to the living room. The hearth still glows, but there is little warmth coming from it. I can make out Antonio's shape. Only his head and torso rest on the small sofa. His legs hang off the side. I shake his shoulder.

He awakens groggy and sits up. He's also in his thermal underwear. His flannel shirt and Levi's hang over the rocking chair, his socks tucked inside his boots.

"What do you need, buddy?" he asks, rubbing his eyes.

"I need you to sleep in your own bed, Antonio. I feel like I kicked you out and can't get to sleep thinking about you all cramped up out here."

"Will you stay with me?" he asks, standing up.

"I'm scared, Antonio," I confess to him.

He takes my hand and places it on his chest where I feel the insistent thumping of his heart. He leads me back to the bedroom.

"Tell you what, Six. We're just going to keep each other warm tonight. We'll keep our longjohns on, all right?"

"OK," I reply. "And how about maybe putting a fence rail down the middle?"

He laughs and pokes my ribs, tickling me. We sit at the edge of the bed. I take my blue bandana from my pile of clothes on the chair. Putting it around the back of Antonio's neck, I pull his head closer and kiss him.

"Feliz Navidad, Antonio," I tell him, tying the kerchief.

He opens the drawer of the night table and takes out a red bandana. He folds it into a triangle and puts it around my neck, tying it beneath my Adam's apple. His fingers are cold.

"Merry Christmas, Six," he says. "Come on. Let's crawl in."

I climb into bed on the other side and scramble beneath

the quilt and covers. The sheets are freezing all over again.

He tickles me again and I tickle him back. A little bit of a wrestling match ensues. The sheets are no longer so cold.

We face each other in the flickering light of the lantern. I see his smile and a twinkle in his eye.

"I had a chum, Tomás, in grade school," Antonio tells me. "We were in Boy Scouts and Tomás and I always shared a pup tent. It got so cold one night we crawled into the same sleeping bag. It was fun. And it got us warm in a hurry."

"That's a nice story on a cold night," I remark. "Good night, Antonio."

"Good night, Six. God bless you."

I turn on my other side so we do not breathe in each other's breath. Antonio nudges up against me, placing his arm around me, his hand resting on my chest. It is such an easy and natural position we find ourselves in. We fit together. I suppose that's why it's called *spooning*.

I feel Antonio's breathing on my neck. It grows shallower and I realize he is asleep.

I am still a bit restless. My mind turns to reciting all the thrilling sensations involved in our intimacy, from unhurried kissing to putting my hand in the ass pocket of Antonio's Levi's—while he's wearing them. I replay each scene.

I slip down into sleep so slowly I do not remember when it happened.

When I bob up to the surface of wakefulness once more, the railroad lantern still flickers on top of the dresser. I am warm and cozy.

Antonio and I have not changed our positions, but he's got quite a boner pushed up against my backside. He's asleep. I push back against him, but it has an effect opposite to my intention. He snuggles closer and emits a throaty noise halfway between purring and growling.

I smile before floating sleepward again.

———————⊃∘⊂———————

Upon my next awakening, Antonio and I have exchanged

positions. I breathe on his neck this time and my boner is pressed up against his butt. I do not pull away.

I wonder what it will feel like to lie next to him naked.

But I do not want to get ahead of myself. I do not have to imagine anything beyond tonight, lying next to my friend Antonio, feeling his warmth, smelling his smell—a combination of piñon and hair oil. I like his smell and, truth be told, it revs my engine.

It is the best Christmas I remember. I drift asleep for the last time before morning, holding onto Antonio and thanking God for bringing these two orphans who had nowhere to go into each other's arms on this snowy, blustery Christmas Eve.

LAS SOMBRAS ERRANTES
THE WANDERING SHADOWS

The shadows of the fence posts march across the scrubby yard. The cross-rails lie rotting on the ground. Each day the hands and fingers of the gnarled cottonwoods reach further into the corral, where the ghosts of my horses, Cornflower and Ferdinand, stare in gray disbelief. One day, when we all lie below the ground, I shall be able to ride them again.

Darkness gathers in the corners of the kitchen as sunset outlines The Mountain in rose and gold. My cup of tea has grown cold. I debate whether it is worth the effort to reheat it on the wood stove. I reach into my apron pocket for a match in case the fire has gone out. I stir the embers and add a tiny log of cedar. Though the smoke rises up through the chimney, the sweet fragrance scents the entire house, the aroma seeping into the plaster.

I watch night fill the yard, the first stars brightening in the moonless sky. There is not enough of interest outside to hold my attention. I go back to composing my guest list at the kitchen table, ignoring my tea in the speckled enamel pot until it has nearly all boiled away. There's barely enough to fill half my cup. The tea is strong. I drop in another sugar cube and stir it with the fork, left from breakfast, that is at hand.

It is only two weeks until the longest night of the year. I prefer to think of it more optimistically as the shortest day of the year. They only grow longer after that.

I light the kerosene lamp on the table rather than switch on the electric light overhead. The ceiling fixture casts such harsh shadows, making me look even older than my eight-eight years.

Though it is not difficult to decide who is to be on the list for my annual Christmas gathering, the faces come to me long before their names. I finger one of my long gray braids.

I think I hear a noise in the yard. Turning down the oil lamp, I stand at the kitchen window, my hands in my apron pockets, peering into the darkness. There is just enough starlight to catch shadows darting about the yard, but they leave no impressions in the fresh snow.

My ancestors footsteps are as soft as the sound of snowflakes falling on snowy ground. Hardly do I think I hear them than they have drifted away. They often play tricks, hiding things on me. I toy with them, too, putting stones on little objects so they cannot lift them. They are the small pranks old friends play on each other who have known one another for lifetimes.

I go back to the table. Turning up the oil lamp, I take up the fountain pen and complete my guest list. My tally comprises everyone I know whose name remains in my address book or whose memory stays lodged in my heart. Not everyone will come. Many are dead.

I don't remember finishing my tea, but the cup is empty. There are rings at the bottom as though it simply evaporated.

Tomorrow I shall look for my good writing paper, envelopes, and three-cent stamps.

———————◦○◦———————

Though I did not expect my husband, Eduardo, to reply to the invitation to my little holiday gathering, I addressed one to him anyhow, as I have every Christmas. It is the time of year I need to forgive him all over again, as many times as it takes.

He left me with an infant daughter and no way to make a living. Eduardo was killed nearly forty years ago, crushed by a stack of lumber that collapsed on him at the sawmill.

We do not ask for most of the disasters which befall us and do not deserve most of the blessings. Yet they both happen.

I got by with the help of my brother, Nicolás, and two of my neighbors who suggested I take in wash like them. I was able, in that way, to earn money and still watch after my daughter, Benita, until she was old enough for school.

The owner of the sawmill sent me money for my daughter's education every year at Christmas for the rest of his life. As a result, Benita is too smart for the neighborhood we live in. She advises any and all exactly what they should do in every situation. She has pushed her own daughter, Nina, away.

I never married again. It did not feel right since I still saw my husband from time to time. His shadow used to hold my hand. It was cold. We had occasional conversations, too, but he had never been much of a talker—like most of the men I know—except for Benita's son, my grandson, Antonio.

I have not heard from my husband in three years now. I believe Eduardo has at last moved on—in answer to my many Christmas prayers.

———————◦———————

It is at last Christmas Eve. Like a child, I didn't believe it would ever get here. My other child's wish has also been granted: that it snow. The snowflakes are huge and light like goose's down. They float in the light of the full moon.

I flip the switch for the electric lights again and again, but they do not go on. Perhaps a winter storm someplace has brought down the power lines. I light every oil lamp and lantern and candle in my little *casita*—the one I intend leaving to my grandson and his *compadre*—Sixtus, his best friend since grade school.

Even with all the tiny flames blazing, the house is not warm. I would have liked to build a fire in my hive-shaped hearth before my guests arrive, but I could not carry the logs, only kindling. I'll have to wait until one of the men of the family shows up.

My brother Nicolás is the first to arrive. His smile is wide, the candlelight flickering on his teeth. He kisses my cheek and I kiss his.

"It's quite cheerful in here, Ana."

"Thank you. I can't get the electric to work."

"Very unreliable," my brother remarks. "That's why I had my electric turned off."

"I thought it got *cut off* because you quit paying your bill."

"*Quit* makes it sound like I didn't pay it on purpose," Nicolás tells me.

I smile so we do not get into an argument on Christmas Eve. After all, each of us knows what we know, even if our accounts of it differ. I love my brother and do not wish to hurt him with my *testarudo*, my stubborn, insistence that I alone am right. We are both right.

"*Feliz Navidad,*" I say. "Merry Christmas, Nicolás."

"Do you have anything to warm the blood on this cold and windy night, dear Ana?"

"Every night seems cold to me lately. I have a bottle of brandy in the kitchen cupboard, but I cannot get the cork out. If you can open it, you may have a small glass. But I want to leave some for my grandson and his friend. They will be chilled coming all this way with the heater in his pickup truck not working."

Nicolás is unable to open the bottle of brandy, either. I wouldn't have minded a small glass myself. I ask him to bring in a couple logs for a fire. He goes out to the woodpile beneath the deep eaves in back, not wearing his coat or scarf or hat. I'm afraid he'll catch a death of cold.

He has worn himself out bringing in a single small log that could not provide more than ten minutes of warmth. He looks frail and unwell to me in the flickering light of the candles. I tell him we shall wait for his grand-nephew, Antonio, to arrive. He and Six will have the place aglow with a fire in no time. My brother and I sit down in a pair of wooden rocking chairs in front of the empty hearth to wait for them.

"Do you think Eduardo will show up this year?" my brother asks.

"I hope not, Nicolás. If he does not come tonight, it will mean he has found his rest. That is my Christmas prayer, though one more visit from him would be nice."

"I understand," my brother says, nodding.

A clattering at the front door tells me my grandson and

his companion have arrived. Their arms are laden with bundles and packages, and each carries a banged-up valise. They set the suitcases down just inside the front door and set their burdens on the coffee table. They do not see me and my brother in the darkest corner of the living room by the cold fireplace. It would be fun to spook them, but we do not.

The electric lights go on in a brilliant flash. The light switch works for *them*. I'm a little annoyed. My grandson hugs his friend and they kiss each other.

"Come," my brother tells me. "I do not care to see two men kissing."

"They love each other. That's what's important," I tell him.

Nicolás tugs my sleeve and we go into the kitchen.

"Don't you remember Tio Jorge and his friend who lived together?" I continue.

"Yes, of course. But I never saw them kiss each other on the mouth."

"You're so old-fashioned."

"I don't mind being old-fashioned."

My grandson enters the kitchen with two shopping bags full of food. It smells delicious.

"There you are," Antonio says. "I knew you had to be here somewhere, with all the candles and lanterns glowing. It looks very festive. *Es muy festivo*, Grandma. Thank you."

He gives me and my brother a kiss on the cheek. My brother does not quite know yet that he is dead. Antonio, who has some of my abilities, must see his great-uncle Nicolás as clearly as he sees me. He is teaching his friend, Sixtus, a little bit of magic, too, but I have no idea how skilled he has become.

"Maybe you could ask your friend to bring in an armload of firewood for us so we can all get warm later," my brother says to Antonio. "You and I and your grandma will stay out here in the kitchen and visit. It's warmer here."

"I'll get the fire going, Tio Nicolás. Six is already hauling in the Christmas tree. Maybe you and Grandma can help us decorate it later—if that's not too much for you, Uncle."

"Of course not," he replies.

"I am so happy we are going to have a Christmas tree, Antonio," I tell my grandson. "God bless you and Six. I did not want to ask you."

"Thanks for the meal, too, Nephew. I'm pretty hungry."

"Hands off, Nicolás," I tell my brother, slapping his hand. "You'll just make a mess of things. You wait until the others have eaten."

"Would you and Six like a little bit of brandy?" I ask my grandson.

"Maybe later. I want to get a fire going and help Six with the tree."

"Would you mind first getting the cork out for us?" Nicolás asks him. "It's stuck."

"All right. But you two go easy. I'm not sure what effect alcohol will have in your condition."

"Of course," my brother says. "Just a little sip or two to warm our bones, that's all."

His remark almost makes me laugh out loud.

Antonio goes out back and returns with an armload of *piñon* logs for the fireplace.

"You two are welcome to join us in the living room whenever you like," my grandson tells us. "You don't have to hide out in here. Six looks forward to seeing you both."

From the kitchen, I see that the fire is soon blazing. Antonio and Six get the Christmas tree upright in its stand. I want to bring water from the kitchen sink for the thirsty evergreen but cannot carry it. I motion to my grandson in the parlor.

"Maybe you can help *mi abuela* carry water for the tree, Six," my grandson says to his friend.

"Sure," he replies. "Where is Grandma? Is she hiding?"

"She's out in the kitchen," Antonio tells him.

Six walks into the kitchen. "God bless you, Grandma," he says. "It is good to see you again, especially at this time of year."

I tell him he is looking very happy and ask him to carry the small bucket of water for the tree sitting in the sink beneath the hand pump.

"Uncle Nicolás," Six says. "I didn't see you there in the corner. It has been a very long time since I saw you."

My brother replies, but I don't think Six can hear him. It is quite remarkable that he can see Nicolás. My grandson is teaching him well. My only regret is that they will not have a child to pass the gift on to.

"Please, Abuela, Tio Nicolás," Six says. "Come join us in the living room. The fire is roaring and it is getting warm and pleasant."

My brother and I follow him into the parlor. Nicolás stands by the fire.

"Look who's here," Six says to Antonio.

"Tio Nicolás. Feliz Navidad," Antonio says to his great-uncle, a bit surprised that Six can see him. "Sit down while we decorate the tree. All advice will be happily ignored."

My brother laughs one of his deep belly-laughs. I think Six must have heard it. He turns to look at Tio Nicolás.

My grandson and his companion dance around one another, weaving in and out as they string the lights on the tree. Six pinches Antonio's rear end on each pass. He thinks I do not see it, but I can see behind things if I want to.

All the electric Christmas tree bulbs are small round ones, all pearly white. The ornaments are either clear or frosted or silver, except for a shining red glass heart exactly where a pine tree would have a heart. I pick up one of the small silver ornaments from the box but drop it on my way across the living room. Six jumps at the sound as though it were a gunshot.

"Don't worry, Grandma," my grandson's friend tells me. "Anything that is used will be broken."

Antonio unpacks my old hand-carved crèche and places it beneath the tree, arranging the figures according to the Christmas story. He comes to sit beside me in the other rocker. I touch his hand.

As Six hangs a single strand of tinsel from the tip of each branch, my grandson points out the ones he's missed. They smile at each other. The light in their eyes outshines the Christmas tree. I am happy to bask in it.

My brother leans against the hearth. I think he's asleep

standing up. If he were more than a shadow, I'd scold him for blocking the warmth, but I think it passes right through him.

I get up from the rocker with difficulty and draw closer to the fire. I rub my hands together, but I don't feel much heat. I ask Six to bring in more firewood. He finishes hanging the last few tinsel icicles and goes out.

"Do you think Mama or Nina will come, Grandma?" my grandson asks me.

"All we can do, Antonio, is invite people into our lives. It is not up to us whether or not they accept. But I have a feeling your Mama will come. She was not very nice to Six last time. I think she wants to make it up to him."

"I hope so," he tells me. "And I hope Nina forgives Mama. I just want everybody I love to get along. Is that asking so much?"

"Sometimes it's asking more than people have in their hearts, *mi amado nieto*—my beloved grandson. We must be patient. Don't worry. Six is always nice to your Mama. He is a kind man. Once the magic of kindness is planted, it only grows."

Six comes back inside with a log-carrier full of wood. He makes a great racket and sets the bundle beside the fireplace. I want to tell him to cast the entire load onto the fire, but he adds just two logs. It's better than nothing.

There is a knock on the front door. Benita does not wait, but barges right in. I scowl at her, but, of course, she does not see it.

"That feels awfully nice," she says, almost pushing me and Nicolás aside in her hurry to stand in front of the fire.

Antonio approaches his mother. He hugs her and kisses her and offers to take her coat. Six offers his Christmas greeting, but she does not hear him, either. She hands over her blazing red coat with white fur trim. She looks like Mrs. Santa Claus.

"Where is José, Mama? I thought he was coming with you?"

"He's gotten to be quite a handful, Antonio—his fearsome fives, I guess. The girl down the road, Hermione, is watching him. I told her to be here at seven. It's quarter past."

"Take it easy, Mama," my grandson tells her. "Maybe the

snow is slowing them down."

"You did a wonderful job decorating the tree, Antonio," she says, changing the subject.

"I only helped with a couple of the lights, Mama. Six did all the rest of it."

"Yes, of course," she says, glancing over at Six and offering a weak smile. "Do you boys need help in the kitchen? Of course you do. Just let me warm up for a minute."

"We have things pretty much under control, Mama Morales," Six tells her. "Please. Get comfortable by the fire."

I am so happy neither Antonio nor Six allows her to push them around. I wish I could have explained that simple procedure to Nina before she ran away. But Nina did not listen to anybody— not even her grandma.

"Would you like a little brandy, Mama Morales? Do you mind if I just call you Mama M.?" Six asks her.

"I'd love a little brandy, Six. Yes, you may call me Mama M. I like the sound of it."

I never thought I'd live to see the day, but my heart sings that it has finally arrived. Benita is being kind to her son's partner.

Six goes out to the kitchen. Antonio and his mother take the rockers by the fire. I don't know where my brother has gotten himself off to. He was looking a little thin tonight—barely visible, even to me.

"Have you and Six talked about your trying to adopt the little one? I know he's crazy about you both. I just cannot do it any longer, Antonio. He wears me out. He needs a man's discipline. Two men will certainly not be too many for that child."

"Six is very much in favor of José coming to live with us, Mama. But the adoption would be a lot easier if we had something from Nina giving him up for adoption."

"Your grandma wrote her a while ago, but then she... well... I don't expect we'll ever hear from Nina again."

"If that's what you believe, Mama, that's what will happen. You must not give up hope, especially at Christmas."

"I suppose you are right," my daughter says. "But it has been three years since she ran off and left me with the little one.

Every Christmas, I hope we'll hear from Nina, and every year is the same disappointment."

"This year is different, Mama. You'll see."

My daughter shrugs her shoulders.

"Is Papa coming?" Antonio asks his mother. There is pleading in his voice like when he was a boy.

"No, I'm afraid not," she replies. "He called from Mexico to tell me he would not be home for Christmas. He's probably with... well... None of my business."

Six enters with four small glasses on a tray and the bottle of brandy.

"Why four glasses? You boys expecting more company?"

"It's for Grandma," Six tells her.

"Don't tell me you see her, too," Benita remarks.

"I do, Mama M. And Tio Nicolás, too. He was asleep by the fire before. I don't know where he went," he says, looking around.

"I'm afraid my son is having a bad influence on you, Six. I thought he'd given up on his silly belief in magic. There's no such thing."

My grandson's companion eases the tension by pouring a little brandy in each of the glasses and proposing a toast.

"*Que vivas durante todos los días de tu vida*," Six says. "May you continue to live all the days of your life."

Six is learning Spanish as well as magic. I laugh a bit too loudly at his toast. My daughter looks up as though she heard me at last.

"That storm is howling tonight," she says instead.

A gust of wind slams against the front door and it bursts open. The neighbor girl and my great-grandson stand at the threshold, bundled up with only their eyes showing. Swirls of snow rush in behind them. My grandson pushes the door shut.

Little José bounds into the room before anyone can remove his coat or galoshes, his cap or scarf or mittens. He runs to his Tio Antonio, whom he addresses as "Papa." Then he runs and hugs Six's knees, whom he calls "Tio Tio." Lastly he comes to his great-grandma, bypassing his Grandma Benita entirely.

Hermione apologizes for unleashing him on us all at once.

She gathers the boy to her and takes off his thick clothes, hanging them on a peg by the door. They look ridiculously tiny.

"Why not stay with us for supper, Hermione?" my grandson says. "We have more than enough," he adds, before she can object.

Antonio is one of the kindest men I know. The babysitter looks around the room. Everyone nods their approval.

"All right," she says, smiling. "Can I help you in the kitchen?"

"I wouldn't mind another pair of hands," Six tells her.

They go off to the kitchen. José toddles after them. He quickly gets into the cupboard for pots and pans and creates a tremendous racket. Six gives him two rubber spatulas and tells him to play the pots like drums—but softly.

'OK, Tio Tio. Like this?"

"Yes. That's better, José. Not too loud. Your grandma is here and loud noises frighten her. Would you like a carrot?"

"Can I put it on the snowman's face?"

"We don't have a snowman yet. Tomorrow we'll make a snowman. I'll be sure to save a carrot for his nose. You can eat that one."

"Thank you, Tio Tio."

I admire Six's patience. The child is a machine for questions. I begin to understand why Benita was not up to taking care of him. I must forgive her.

Hermione takes my decorated Talavera platters from the cupboard. I hold my breath. She might drop one. I go back to the living room so I do not have to watch.

My brother, Nicolás, has dissolved into the corner by the fireplace. Only a little bit of his shadow remains, like a smudge of ashes.

My grandson turns to me and smiles. His mother ignores me.

"When do you and Six plan to move in here?" my daughter asks.

"Grandma said we can move in any time. Six and I brought some of our clothes tonight. But we don't want her to feel unwelcome in her own house."

"Doesn't she know?"

"Don't I know what, Benita?" I ask her.

"I'm sorry, dear. I thought your grandma knew and was just being stubborn."

"Know what?" I ask.

"You must tell her she's dead, Antonio."

"I'll tell her after supper, Mama," my grandson says, winking at me.

I was beginning to have my suspicions that I might be dead when I needed magic to light a candle and had to recite a magic "recipe" just to carry a couple of logs. I also noticed that people ignored me a lot more than they used to, even those with good hearing.

There is a metallic clamor coming from the kitchen. The five-year-old is doing his best imitation of a dinner bell by banging the lids of two pots together. Six has left an empty chair at the table for me, like the one Jewish people leave at Passover for Eijah. I'm glad Nicolás left before he caused a commotion at the table.

The meal is quite a feast. There's a huge pot of *posole* simmering on the stove and breaded fish, Six's Christmas custom. Tomato and green onion salad, and two burritos swimming in melted cheese and green chili sauce, adorn each plate. A bowl of sour cream sits in the center of the table.

Little José notes that my plate is empty. He takes two tiny pieces of black olive from his burrito and puts them on my plate.

He looks up at me and smiles.

"They are for you," he says. "I have too many."

His sweetness and kindness bring a tear to my eye. I realize that my grandson and his friend do indeed have a child worthy of passing our gift to. I am happy beyond measure.

The food at the table disappears faster than if it had been set upon by a pack of wolves. Hermione and Antonio clear the table. There are cherry jack *empanadas* with green chilies and *sopapillas* with honey for dessert. José has a sweet-tooth like me and pours more honey all over his puffy pastry. He is sticky enough to hang on the wall.

I excuse myself and go out to the parlor, settling onto the pillow-strewn *banco* beside the fireplace. There is not a trace of my brother.

The crowd from the kitchen reassembles in the living room, led by José. The boy dives beneath the Christmas tree. He begins playing with the carved figures in the Nativity scene, telling himself his own stories. He places baby Jesús on one of the wise men's camels and has the Magus palaver with the angel on the roof of the stable.

Antonio brings the bottle of my brandy, offering a little nip to the three adults. Hermione is too young. I'd like a sip, too, but it is enough for me just to smell the aged brandy. It brings a smile to my lips recalling all the occasions the liquor has brought a smile to the lips of my guests and warmth to their hearts. The bottle seems never to run out.

While the grown-ups enjoy their brandy, I tell José the story of his namesake in the crèche who carries a *farolito*, a small lantern. He sits rapt as I tell him about the Holy Family's long journey and about the inns of Bethlehem that were too full for even baby Jesús and his Mama and Papa.

José nods. "Yes," he tells me. "Papa said they had to go sleep in the barn with the donkey."

"That's right, my child. That is where little Jesús was born."

I hope Antonio and Six keep up the tradition of the *posada* in which the tale is re-enacted throughout the neighborhood.

Antonio fetches a beautiful wool shawl for his Mama from him and Six. The colors, in traditional Southwest patterns, are radiant. She thanks both her boys and showers them with kisses. A folded sheet of paper falls from the shawl as she throws it over her shoulders.

"What's this?" she asks, unfolding the paper.

She reads, and then bursts into tears, the joyful kind.

"You must let me help with this, Antonio," she tells her son.

"That's not necessary, Mama. Six and I saved our pennies for the lawyer. He said that, because I am José's closest relative willing to take him in, it's a pretty straightforward adoption. You are on the papers only as a back-up, in case something happens to me."

"You boys make me so happy. And proud. Little José is very lucky to have two papas who love him."

"Yes," the boy tells his grandma. "I am lucky as a pig in mud," he says, grinning.

"Well, something like that," Six remarks. "We have a present for you, José, from your papa and me. Then you have to go to bed so Santa will come."

Six hands the boy the rather inexpertly-wrapped package. He tears into it like a dog digging. Just as well it wasn't wrapped too fancy.

It is a tablet of drawing paper and a box of twenty-four Crayolas.

"Oh, boy," he shouts, opening the pack of crayons and calling out their colors.

"He does so well with coloring books, we thought we'd see how he does making his own pictures," Six tells Benita.

"You draw only on the paper, José," my grandson tells him. "Any crayon marks we find someplace else and we'll have to melt the crayons down and make a candle out of them."

"Can I watch?" the boy asks.

Six and Antonio and my daughter smile secretly to one another. I am happy my great-grandson has an inquisitive nature.

"If you climb on my back, I'll take you to bed. Kiss your grandma and your uncle good night," Antonio tells him.

"Am I staying overnight?" the boy asks. "Where will I sleep?"

"Your bed is in back, José, in your own room. It used to be the back porch, remember? Now it is your room—your very own bedroom."

"Is it dark in there?" my great-grandson asks.

"Yes. It's night time. But your Tio is letting you use his lantern, his *farolito*. That will keep you safe."

"OK," he says. "Giddy up, Papa. Good night, Grandmama," he says to me, blowing me a kiss over my grandson's shoulder. "Faster, Papa. I have spurs on."

Antonio returns with a package hastily wrapped in white tissue paper. His bedtime story for José was a long one.

"His horse had to tell him a cowboy story first," Antonio says. "This is for you, Hermione," he adds, handing her the small gift. "In his excitement tonight, José forgot to give it to you."

The sweet girl blushes and unwraps the gift, trying not to tear the paper—as though she might reuse it. My grandson has given her one of my hand-embroidered aprons. *Just as well,* I think. I can't picture either Antonio or Six wearing that apron.

Hermione thanks my grandson and shakes Six's hand. She says it is nearly nine o'clock and she should be getting home.

"I'll drive you home, child," my daughter tells her. "First, there's one more gift to hand out."

A knock at the front door startles us all. Antonio opens it. A swirl of wind and snow blusters in. It is Nicolás, dressed as a U. S. Postal carrier. His cap is pulled down low over his eyes. I am the only one who recognizes him.

"Special Delivery for Mrs. Benita Morales," he announces.

My brother looks more substantial than he has in a while. His voice is loud and clear, too. He must have been saving up his energy for this. That would explain his looking so weak and faded all evening.

Benita accepts the large envelope from her Tio Nicolás whom she does not recognize. Her hands tremble as she tears the manila envelope open.

"It is from Nina," she says, her voice catching, tears rolling down her cheeks.

"See?" my grandson tells his mother. "I knew we would hear from her this Christmas."

There are many pages attached with a big paper clip. Benita reads the hand-written cover page aloud.

Dear Mama,

Merry Christmas and God bless you.
I am so sorry for my bad behavior. It was
wrong of me to saddle you with José without saying

anything.

> *Grandma told me how hard it has been for you. I do not want the little one to be sent to live with strangers. She told me Antonio and his companion are willing to adopt José. How wonderful! It makes me so happy!*

> *I understand the boy loves his Tio and his Tio's friend. He will have two papas.*

> *The other papers are from the lawyer who drew them up for José's adoption. They must be signed and returned, and then things can move forward.*

> *I am leaving Geraldo, Mama, as soon as I can get someplace where he will not find me.*

> *Happy New Year!*

My love to everyone, but especially to you, Mama.

Nina

My daughter holds the letter against her breast. She sits down near the fire. Six brings her a glass of water and a little bit of brandy. She leans forward to kiss him.

I am the only one who notices my brother, the mailman, has left—without even opening the door.

"Where's the special delivery guy?" Antonio asks. "I wanted to give him a couple dollars."

Everyone looks around and shrugs their shoulders. Benita hands the sheaf of papers to her son and his friend, infecting them with her excitement.

"Dear Six," Benita tells her son's friend. "I'm so sorry for the way I have treated you. It was shameful. You belong to my son. You are my second son."

She takes hold of his hands and gives him a small package wrapped in plain brown paper and a ribbon of red yarn.

"Though the present is for both of you," my daughter says, "it is to you, Six, that I give it—with all my apologies for being such a mother-in-law."

We all laugh and she hugs the boys. I am happy Benita has turned around before it is too late. It is the best Christmas present I could have received.

"Thank you, Benita," I tell her. "Feliz Navidad," I shout so she'll hear me.

She looks up, right where I am standing. I peer around Six's shoulder as he and Antonio unwrap the tiny package. Their hands tremble with anticipation.

"Mama. I don't know what to say," Antonio tells his mama.

Six is so dumbfounded he cannot get even that much out.

"They came from a fellow on the Pueblo, a metalsmith who makes the most *magical* jewelry," Benita tells them.

I never expected my daughter to use the word magical except as a disparaging term.

"The old man always asks who is to receive the items he makes, what the person likes, and what the occasion is. So I told him everything. He made them especially for you two. It's pure copper. He said that was the right metal for men who love men."

Antonio and Six hug Benita. She kisses them both on the cheek.

"They are so perfect, Mama M. The snake chasing its tail is one of our favorite symbols."

"I'm not sure I would wear them in public, though," my daughter adds, nearly erasing all the goodwill she's recently built up with me.

"Why, Mama? All our friends know who me and Six are. I want to show off my ring. It is so beautiful. And it reminds me of my bond with Six."

"I suppose you are right, dear. Do you remember my Tio Jorge and his friend who lived together?"

"Of course I remember them: a funny pair of old coots, always dressed like a couple of prospectors."

"What do you think we're going to be like when we're old men?" Six asks my grandson.

"I refuse to dress like a gold-digger," he replies.

"I think you mean a gold-miner, dear," my daughter says. They laugh.

"You boys should do whatever you feel comfortable doing. Everyone knew what Tio Jorge and his companion were to each other and no one said a word. They were loved by our entire village. You don't need my advice any longer."

"Thank you, Benita," I say, though only Antonio and Six hear me. "It was about time you got around to saying that. God bless you. God bless you all. I'm going to say good night. I promised Nicolás that I'd spend Christmas Eve with him."

"Good night, Grandma," my grandson says, blowing a kiss to me.

"We will miss you," Six says, smiling a sad smile.

I decide to look in on little José before taking my leave. He is cocooned into the covers with only his nose visible. I touch his forehead in blessing. Then I walk through the wall of the boy's tiny bedroom and stand in the back yard.

I cast no more shadow in the icy moonlight than the tendrils of smoke rising from the chimney. The snow is silent beneath the soles of my hand-knit slippers, as though I weigh nothing. Surprisingly, I am not cold. I see the exquisite detail of each sparkling snowflake as it tumbles past me in the silvery light. Time moves like an old horse.

In the distance, I make out Nicolás, leaning against a tree in the same posture as when I last saw him propped against the fireplace. He looks entirely substantial here, though I can see he's holding a lit cigarette behind his back.

"You may as well go ahead and smoke it, Nicolás. It's not going to do you any harm now. You're already dead."

My brother and I laugh. I take his arm.

"I wasn't sure you were going to come tonight, Ana. You were having such a good time with the family."

"I promised you I would come, Nicolás. Besides, I had my time down there."

We come to a clearing in the woods, in the center of which is a beautifully-shaped Christmas tree lighted with wax candles like I remember as a girl. Their flickering flames dodge the snowflakes.

"Merry Christmas, Ana."

We admire the magical evergreen tree for some time.

"We are like wandering shadows, Nicolás," I tell my brother, "the living and the dead. But I am grateful for everyone whose shadow has fallen across my path."

Nicolás smiles and takes my arm again.

"Come. This way, Ana. Mother and father are just up the road. They're waiting for us."

CHRISTMAS PRESENT

A boy lives across the road. He is around ten years old and is confined to an old-fashioned wheelchair with a cane seat and back. His handler, dressed always in a white blouse and skirt—and even white shoes and stockings and a cap—pushes him up and down the wooden ramp to his front porch. She must be his nurse. The woman is forever stopping and tossing the boys hands back in his lap, I suppose so he does not catch his dangling fingers in the spokes.

Though I swore I'd never allow myself to wind up in a beige, pissy-smelling room, here I am in a nursing home. I complain about my lot, but I had, up until my stroke, a life rich in experiences and full of loving friends, with just a few cantankerous relatives tossed into the pot for spice. I needed only my own steam-power to get around all those years. I can't imagine an existence utterly dependent on the mercy of others as the boy seems to be. Surely I would have killed at least one of them by now.

I've lived here at Valhalla Manor only a short while. I don't know whether the boy across the road has ever walked nor if he can talk. I've watched the boy and his keeper with my old pair of navy binoculars. I have never seen the boy's mouth move.

My window faces west; the boy's looks east. On some days we seem to spend all the daylight hours of short winter afternoons glancing over at one another across the road. I admit my sight is not what it once was. He looks a little like me at that age, though he is darker, his hair black. I am fairer, my hair blond—at least what remains of it.

The boy and I turn away whenever we think the other is watching. It is something of a game not to get caught looking. He's better at it.

I'd like to learn the boy's name before I die. I'm not sure why it's important. Just his first name will do.

Today my nurse wheeled me up to my window and put the brake on like I was going to drive it over the sill. But she never parted the curtains. I faced the ugly pattern of chickens and roosters and a maid casting corn at them from a bucket. I don't like complaining except to myself, but I never encountered a stupider person in eighty-eight years. That takes some doing.

This is not the first time my nurse has parked me in front of the drawn curtains. I don't know whether to burst into tears or burst into flames. How could I even explain it to her without singeing her hair? Instead, I think of ways I might communicate with the boy across the road.

My first thought is a surplus signal lamp like we used aboard ship. They are large and expensive and the Valhalla Manor Nursing Home administrator probably wouldn't let me have one in my room. It's doubtful the boy knows Morse code and wouldn't be able to decode my messages. He'd need a blinker light, too, in order to signal me back.

The distance across the road isn't too great to stretch a string attached to tin cans on either end. But who was I going to get to hang the string twenty feet above the ground? Maybe I could attach the can at the other end to something heavy—a stone perhaps—and toss the can and string across the road to the boy's window. Truth be told, however, I've always been a lousy pitcher. No one ever wanted me on their team. I'd probably smash the boy's window.

What if I caught a crow outside my window and attached one end of the string to his foot and sent him across the road? But who knows where the crow would take off to? It'd take months to train the bird. I don't know if I have even five minutes left before I check out.

Maybe a carrier pigeon will land at my window and I'll

attach my message to his leg and send him to the boy. But, wait. Aren't carrier pigeons extinct? *No,* I think, *it's passenger pigeons that have died out.* I'm not sure.

There is the United States Postal Service as a last resort, but I don't know the boy's address. I can't even remember the name of the road I live on—if you can call this living.

I fall asleep in my wheelchair before my brain manages to cook up any more useless notions about how to communicate with the boy across the road.

I awaken with the idea in my head to draw large letters of the alphabet. They offer so-called art classes here at Valhalla to keep the inmates out of trouble. When the teacher—I forget her name—sees what I'm up to, she tells me, "Not very original, Mr. Thorson. It's been done before."

"Not like this," I tell her. "I plan on using every color of the rainbow for this alphabet."

"The tempera paints come in only the primary colors, plus white and black. You'll have to mix them."

"OK. Maybe you can show me, Miss... uh... Did you know that rainbows don't actually exist, that they aren't really there? Yet everybody sees them."

"Fascinating, Mr. Thorson. Please pay attention."

The art teacher launches into a lecture about color theory for the rest of the hour of class. It's not a theory to me. It's either a certain color or it isn't. I decide my alphabet doesn't need to be that fancy. Miss So-and-So offers her critique, but I'm not interested. I remind her plain old black was good enough for Henry Ford's first cars. It's good enough for my alphabet.

I manage to get three or four letters done each art class, twice a week. Once I decide I probably won't need Q, Z, and X anytime soon, I'm nearly ready to start transmitting messages to the boy across the road.

One sunny afternoon, when the boy's nurse wheels him to

his perch by the window, I send him my first message. My window is wide and tall enough that I can tape four letters across and three letters down. I'd made off with a roll of masking tape when the old guy next door shuffled off his mortal coil and they repainted his room. I realize I should have made duplicates of certain letters.

"H-E-L-O," I signal, sticking the letters to the glass.

Peering with my binoculars, I see the boy is looking across at me and up at the sign. I don't expect him to answer me today. He'll have to get his hands on some paper and crayons, and draw his own alphabet.

The boy moves his hand in a circle. I'm not sure what he means. He does it again, the other way around, and points to my sign in the window.

He's telling me to arrange the letters the other way around, I guess. From outside, on the other side of the street, the letters are in reverse order and the words are spelled backwards.

I'm going to have a busy couple of days in art class drawing the missing letters and making a few duplicates. But which ones?

I decide to leave my sign up even after the boy has been wheeled away. My nurse-keeper comes in.

"The director has complained about your signs in the window," she says, pulling them down.

She draws the ugly curtains and leaves my room. She heads down the hall to annoy someone else.

Supper will be coming soon. I know I'm not supposed to like it, but I think the food at Valhalla Manor isn't half-bad. It beats anything I made at home after Mildred died.

By the time I've drawn a few duplicate letters of the alphabet, some numbers, and a question mark, it's only two days before Christmas. I wonder whether the boy and I will figure out how to have a conversation. He seems more interesting than any of the geezers and biddies on my floor.

The boy is already sitting at his window by the time a different nurse, not my usual one, wheels me to my window and parts the curtains. She tells me her name but it goes in one ear and out the other without encountering any resistance.

I tape up the letters in backwards order so it will make sense from outside, spelling *H-E-L-O* once again.

H-I, the boy signs back.

I like the lad. He doesn't waste words or letters.

Taking down my greeting, I put up, *N-A-M-E*. The question mark has to go on the next line. The boy's letters are smaller. He gets six of them across. I can still decipher them without my binoculars.

A-D-A-M, he replies.

I'd like to tell him, "Good thing it's not *Nabuchadnezzar*," but he's already written me back.

Y-O-U-R-S-? he asks.

S-I-X, I reply.

6-W-H-A-T-?

N-A-M-E__I-S-S-I__X-T-U-S, I say, using up all three lines and filling the window. I hope my having only four letters to a line won't throw him

W-H-A-T__H-A-P-E-N-D__2-U-? Adam asks.

His abbreviations show he's a clever kid.

S-T-R-O__K-E, I reply.

Then I ask, *A-N-D-U_?*, again putting the question mark on the next line.

P-O-L-I-O, Adam replies.

S-O-R-Y, I say.

N-O-T-Y-U-R__F-A-U-L-T, he writes.

W-H-E-N__? I ask.

W-H-E-N__W-H-A-T-? Adam replies.

P-O-L-I-O, I say, cramming the *I* between the other letters.

2-Y-E-A-R-S, he responds.

We carry on in that fashion for the rest of the afternoon. I learn Adam is not living in his parents' house. Like me, he's living in a nursing home. The place across the road is called the Saint Giles' Home for the Crippled. I didn't see the sign because I face it edge on.

The boy was afflicted with polio two summers ago when he turned eight. He's been told he will not walk again without the aid of braces on both legs and crutches. His classmates from school and playmates from his neighborhood never come to see him. His mother and father visit often, but it's a long drive from Albuquerque where they live. Adam's as alone as I am.

The sun sets long before we have finished our across-the-road correspondence. Adam is wheeled away by his nurse while I remain at my window.

I feel very sad. Though the sunset is brilliantly imbued with hues of orange and rose and gold, it is a sad sunset. I think of the many things the boy will not get to experience. He will not run again, or play football and chase after girls.

My own life has been stuffed to bursting with the countless things I have gone through in my day, from my many lifelong friends and lovers to all the things I've learned from them. It's enough to cram two lifetimes full of joy and sadness. I have no regrets. There's nothing I left undone, nothing I wish I'd gotten around to. I hope Adam will be able to say as much when his time nears.

When my nurse brings my breakfast of cold oatmeal and stewed prunes, there's a small package and a letter on the tray.

"From the boy across the way," she tells me, parking my wheelchair in front of the tray table.

"Thank you," I say, adding, "Merry Christmas."

She smiles at me, an occurrence so uncommon around here I want to ask her if she's feeling well. I suppose my *Thank yous* might be just as rare.

Of course I rip into the package before reading the letter. The Christmas paper has been drawn by hand with crayons. I hate to tear the paper, but the package is, after all, supposed to be opened.

It is an olive drab flashlight, the kind where the light bulb is at a ninety-degree angle to the compartment that holds the batteries. There's a clip to fasten it to your belt and a little button to flash the beam on and off quickly. I have one already, an old government-issue flashlight from my days in the United States Navy.

Mine has dents and scratches; the boy's—the one he sent me—looks new. Maybe he got it in Cub Scouts before he got polio.

I choke down my breakfast. Then I open the letter from Adam. It has arrived with no stamp, written on a sheet of lined paper folded to become its own envelope.

Mr. Sixtus van Thorson
on 2ND floor
Valhalla Nursing home
Red Willow, new Mexico

Dear Mr. Sixtus,

Thank you for being my friend. You are very interesting and I like you.

I have already spoken with you more in two days than I have with anyone in the last two years.

Don't worry. I have a second flashlight to signal you back. My chum at school never got the hang of it.

Merry Christmas.

Sincerely,
Adam

P. S. I hope you know Morse code. If not, I will teach it to you.

That's rich, I think. *He's going to teach* me *Morse code.*

Not knowing when lunch and supper might be served on a holiday, I make sure I finish my breakfast tray. I carefully smooth out and fold Adam's wrapping paper and try out the flashlight. It works, bright enough to see in daylight.

Rummaging through the small chest of drawers in my room, I find my own flashlight tucked in among my longjohns and winter socks. It still works, too. I wrap my note around the flashlight with a rubber band and get my nurse, Audrey, to take it across the road for me. *Hah. I remember her name.* She compliments me on finishing my prunes.

Master Adam Sanchez
2nd Floor east
Saint Giles' Home for Cripples
Red Willow, New Mexico

Dear Adam,

I would very much like to be your friend. You are a smart and upstanding young man.

I will set my mind the task of figuring out how we can meet before this year runs out.

M-E-R-Y__X-M-A-S.

Your friend,
Six

P. S. That flashlight went through World War II with me. We've both got some history.

Once the note has left my hands, I chide myself for calling Adam *upstanding*. He's going to think I'm making fun of him. *No he's not, you old fool,* I tell myself. *He's still innocent of the world.*

By lunchtime, the sky has clouded over and light snow falls, coating everything with a sparkling layer. I decide I'm not going to think about the mud and dirt beneath it.

Audrey brings me a hot chicken sandwich with potato chips. On the side is a glittery green-and-red sugar cookie shaped like a Christmas tree with a yellow star at the top.

"I baked them myself, Mr. Thorson. Yours is the only one that didn't break."

"Is that so?" I remark. "My luck must be changing."

"If you believe so, then it will indeed change, Mr. Thorson," she replies.

I put down the sandwich and reach for the sugar cookie.

"No you don't," Audrey says, gently slapping my hand. "Finish your chicken sandwich first. The *biscochito* is for dessert."

She looks down at me over her glasses and leaves my room. I want to defy her in the worst way for telling me how to eat my lunch, but it's nice being on her good side for a change. I glance across the road. It is snowing harder. Adam is not at his window. I finish my lukewarm sandwich.

When my nurse returns, she stands beside my tray table with her hands on her hips.

"What's wrong with the cookie, Mr. Thorson? You haven't taken even a nibble. It's not like you. Is your sweet tooth off for the holidays?"

"Not very likely," I reply. "I was wondering, Audrey. Would you be offended if I gave your *biscochito* to someone else? As a gift, you understand."

"Depends on who. Yes, I am a little bit offended. It was my Christmas gift to you, Mr. Thorson. My daughter helps me bake them. It's my custom here at Valhalla Manor."

"I'd like to give it to the boy across the road, to Adam."

"I understand. That would be very nice, Mr. Thorson," she says, smiling. "I wish I had another cookie. I could drop it off to the boy on my way home at five o'clock."

"But don't say it came from me, Audrey. Tell him you baked it specially for him."

"He'll know you had something to do with it. He seems a bright boy—and such an unfortunate one," she adds, clicking her tongue.

Audrey takes my tray away, leaving the cookie on the table where it continues to tempt and taunt me. She returns with a piece of Christmas paper and some red ribbon. She hands me a tiny notecard. I get the *To:* and *From:* ass backwards, but she doesn't notice.

"Thank you, Audrey. Bless you. Have a Merry Christmas."

"I already have, Mr. Thorson. It warmed my heart to see you so generous. I know you wanted to eat that cookie yourself. Merry Christmas, dear."

My nurse tucks the tray table in the corner and wheels me to the window. I do not have to remind her to part the ugly curtains. She takes the wrapped cookie with her. I decide to enjoy a brief after-lunch snooze.

When I awaken, Adam is at his perch. He signals me with my Navy flashlight—with *his* Navy flashlight. It is near sundown and the beam illuminates a shaft of snowflakes.

"Helo," he flashes.

"Helo," I reply, using my new Boy Scout flashlight.

Audrey crosses the road in her heavy gray winter coat and shawl, wearing tall decorated mukluks on her feet. Someone at the St. Giles' Home takes the package from her, bowing to her in greeting, a gesture Audrey returns.

I watch Adam's window but do not signal him. The overhead light goes on in his room and the small gift is placed in his lap. The boy looks up at me.

Grabbing my binoculars from the top of my dresser, I watch Adam carefully unwrap the package as though he were planning to reuse the Christmas paper. My mother used to do that. It drove everyone crazy waiting for her to catch up with the rest of the family opening presents.

Adam holds the decorated Christmas *biscochito* in his hands. I want to see him bite the golden star off the evergreen tree. Instead, he closes his eyes. With my binoculars, I see tears stream down his face.

"Thank you, Mr. Six," he flashes. "Best Xmas present ever. And I like the official Navy flashlight, too. Wow. From World War II. It must be worth a lot. Thanks."

His Morse code is flawless; mine's a little rusty, like the ship I served on.

"You have to eat the cookie," I tell him.

"I will, but I want to look at it first."

Our flashlight beams in the heavy snow look like two fire-flies trying to signal each other through thick fog.

"Got any ideas how we can get to meet?" I ask him.

"Not yet," Adam replies. "How about you?"

"I thought we could pull the fire alarms on our floors at the same time. Tomorrow after breakfast, say at nine-thirty. They'd wheel us all out to the curb. It'd be like a block party."

I see the boy laugh.

"We'd get in trouble," he signals. "Someone might get hurt. We might get kicked out."

"Fine with me," I want to tell him, but I don't. Instead, I say, "Good thing one of us is an adult."

Adam laughs again. He picks up the Christmas tree cookie and bites off the star. My mouth waters.

"I could tell them my grandfather was visiting," he flashes. "They'd get me downstairs to the parlor at least."

In the last smudges of sunset, I see he continues to munch his cookie. He's nearly devoured the whole thing already.

"I could say my grandson planned to drive me someplace. They'd at least wheel me down to the curb. I'm old enough to cross the street and back on my own."

I realize Adam would be closer in age to my great-grand-son—if I had one.

"You think you'd make it across OK, Gramps?" he asks.

I realize he's teasing me, like friends do to one another.

"Sure. I'll eat every bean they feed me instead of leaving them on the plate. My wheelchair will be rocket-propelled."

Again the boy flashes, "Ha-ha-ha-ha."

It is too dark to see anything but the signals from his flash-light. They'll be coming to put me to bed soon. There's one more thing I want to tell him.

"Thank you for being my friend, Adam. It's a very special gift. No one ever gave me his friendship for Christmas before."

"Me, either," he replies. "You are my best friend, Mr. Six."

"Pretty low standards, kid."

"No. My standards are high. You are my only friend, and, therefore, the best friend I've got."

"OK," I reply. "What do you say we try to meet this Friday morning?"

"All right. But how will you get back?"

"Just save up the fastest *frijoles* you've got. I'll do the rest."

"M-E-R-Y__X-M-A-S," he signals.

"M-E-R-Y__X-M-A-S, Adam," I say, as the night nurse wheels me away from my window.

She has placed my supper on the tray table. I thank her and ask her name, forgetting it at once. I'm almost too excited about meeting Adam to finish my supper of roast chicken and mashed potatoes with gravy, but I do anyway.

MY LAST CHRISTMAS

My boyfriend has enough Christmas spirit in his heart for both of us. I want to tell him this year is the last time I want to celebrate Christmas. It would really disappoint him, though. I don't want to hurt his feelings.

It's not that I dislike the winter holiday season itself. But everyone I find obnoxious and phony the rest of the year seems even more so at Yuletide. I wish I could take a potion the first Sunday in Advent and not wake up until the Three Kings have remounted their sturdy camels.

Though Six says he's open to suggestions on decorating our tree, I wouldn't dream of telling him where to fasten each light or hang an ornament. He never likes a single one of my ideas anyhow—not because I'm a woman, but because he enjoys Christmas and I emphatically do not. He's tried for the five years we've lived together to bring me over to his camp. I've gotten close, but I've never crossed the line into enemy territory. Perhaps *enemy* is too strong a word. Let's call it *hostile* territory: hostile to my peace of mind.

I watch the festive lights in the shop windows twinkle in Six's eyes. I feel, when he and I are walking down the *Paseo*, that I'm holding the hand of a six-foot, two-inch blond-haired boy. My family came from Mexico and I'm nearly his opposite: brown-skinned and black-haired.

Six's name is short for *Sixtus*, inherited from his Norwegian great-grandfather. I use the cumbersome moniker only when

I'm mad at him. For his sake, I try to curtail that at this time of year. He didn't invent Christmas, after all. I blame Dickens and Albert and Victoria for starting the whole unjolly business—but especially for the custom of greeting cards.

This year, after a joyful hiatus, I heard from Claude and Cynthia Morass. I hadn't received a Christmas card from them since moving to Red Willow ten years ago—a tradition I'd have preferred to keep. My luck had run out.

I open the Morasses' card after returning from yoga. The glittery sparkles get all over my black exercise pants. A newsletter and photo fall out. Their kids, identified on the back of the photo, are just as ugly and buck-toothed as their mother. Their father is no prize-package, either.

The newsletter would have been a grammarian's delight in which every error it is possible to make in English syntax is represented on a single page. It was so uninteresting I recall nothing of its purported "news" except that somebody's pet turtle had "puppies." I start the fire with the newsletter and tuck the greeting card behind the others on the narrow ledge above the hive-shaped hearth.

Six bangs his way into the living room, kicking the back door open and shut with his boot. His cheeks are red and a smile lights up his face. He carries a stack of boxes excavated from the back of the old barn we call our garage. There's never been enough space in it for his old turquoise pickup truck or even my VW Beetle.

The gleam in Six's eyes tells me he has again been infected with the Christmas "bug."

"You're not going to believe what I found, Hypatia," he says, setting the boxes down on the built-in *banco* beside the fireplace.

"A diamond engagement ring?" I reply, never missing an opportunity.

"No," he says, smiling, his cheeks dented by his enormous dimples.

"How about a ring from a Cracker Jack box then?"

"Don't think so," he replies, repeating his display of dimples. "I found stuff that belonged to my *oldefar*—my great-grandfather."

Six wraps his arms around me and plants a long, slow kiss on my lips.

"Why ruin our luck, Hypatia?" he tells me. "We get along as well as any married couple I know. What more could we want?"

"To make it official," I tell him. "To be reminded each time we look at our hands who we belong to."

"Well, we'll see," he says, his usual infuriatingly noncommital answer.

He goes back to the stack of boxes, all marked "Xmas." They look old enough to have come over on the *Mayflower*—if not aboard the *Niña*.

My boyfriend takes off his flannel-lined denim jacket and gloves. No matter how cold and windy and inclement, I have never seen Six wear a hat or even a cap. The only thing he wears on his head, usually in summer as protection from the sun, is his cowboy hat.

He unties the twine on the topmost box and opens it, removing an ancient-looking string of Christmas tree lights with old-fashioned porcelain sockets. The sides of the box are wood.

"These belonged to my *oldefar*, the first Sixtus. I haven't seen them in years."

Six gently untangles the string of lights and drapes it over a couple branches near the top of our fresh evergreen. The light bulbs are about the size of walnuts.

"These actually belonged to a friend of my great-grandfather. I remember their story. They knew each other back when they both worked for the railroad here in New Mexico before it was even a state. They stayed in touch until his friend, Edward, was killed in an electrical accident."

"That doesn't speak well for his string of lights, does it?" I remark. "Was it the Kansas Pacific Railway they worked for by any chance?"

"I'm not sure what the 'electrical accident' was that killed *Oldefar's* friend. Yes, it was the Kansas Pacific. Do you always have to be so smart?"

"No, but knowledge helps me appreciate things in ways I

otherwise might not."

"How about Christmas?"

"I will never understand Christmas."

"Then maybe you haven't asked the right questions, Hypatia."

Six takes a short electrical cord from the pocket of his denim jacket. It is attached to a small metal box.

"*Oldefar's* friend Edward—Edward Hibberd Johnson— later worked with Thomas Edison, so this string of lights he made are direct current. I have to hook them up to the AC transformer from my old train set. Boy, I miss my old Lionel."

I bet he does. He's never quite outgrown his boyhood. But I've decided to be nice this Christmas. Six is anything but an inexperienced boy in the bedroom.

He screws the string of lights into a socket adapter and then plugs the socket into the converter. I want to grab his ass, but contain myself. The other end of the converter he plugs into the wall outlet. The hook-up looks unsafe. The lights flicker for a few seconds and then come on steady. They are red, white, and blue.

"Did this string of lights hang on the White House tree or something?" I ask.

"No, the first electric lights on the White House tree came much later, in 1895, when Grover Cleveland was president."

"His first administration or the second?" I ask, though it doesn't matter which.

"That was during Cleveland's second term," Six says, fastening the first light to a branch near the top of the tree. He does not need to use the stepladder.

"*Do you always have to be so smart?*" I ask him.

"*No, but knowledge helps me appreciate things in ways I otherwise might not,*" he replies, quoting me.

"Touché," I say. "Is that all the lights there are, Six? That won't be nearly enough."

"There are eighty bulbs on this set, Hypatia. That'll be plenty. Mr. Johnson wired this string of lights himself by hand— the first string of electric Christmas tree lights in the whole world. He made them in 1882 and they still work. And they'll be hanging on *our* tree this year."

Six stretches the string of lights around to the back of the tree and attaches a blue light. He's careful not to have two bulbs of the same color hanging too near each other. He peers at me through the branches.

"Aren't you even a little bit impressed, Hypatia, with how old they are?"

"I suppose if I worked at it I might be," I tell him, trying to break into a smile. "I'm sorry, Six. I know you put your heart into Christmas."

"If you'd try to get into the spirit—even a little—you might be surprised what happens."

"I promise I'll try for your sake, Six. You've got two white ones kind of close together down at the bottom. See? There," I say, pointing.

"There's a reason for that, Hypatia," he tells me. "They're there to light up the crèche."

I am about to ask whether he has in mind the primitive and poorly-painted Nativity scene his father carved, but I stop myself.

"Maybe some of your *glögg* will help get me in the proper spirit, Six. Four o'clock's not too early, is it?"

"No, of course not. It's Christmas Eve. Warm up a glass for me, too. I want to keep going with the Christmas tree. I'm hoping to finish before supper."

Six winks at me and turns on his dimpled smile. I go into the kitchen.

I pour some of his homemade spiced liquor into an enameled pot and light the stove. Turning the gas down so the alcohol won't boil off, I take a pair of clear glass coffee mugs from the cupboard. The *glögg* is fragrant and fruity, reminding me of an autumn farm stand.

I suggested to Six that we might want to eat out this Christmas Eve instead of cooking at home. I said we could try the new Cambodian restaurant in town called Pol's Pot that I'd heard so many raves about. Six wrinkled his nose. I know he will insist on preparing his usual family delicacy of *lutefisk*—a kind of pickled fish—with boiled potatoes. And probably something with lingon-berries in it or on it. At least his other holiday custom of making *glögg* is one I enjoy.

Using the soup ladle to spoon the hot spiced mixture into the glass mugs, I place them on a tray. Six has bought some gin-gerbread cookies. I put the cookie men on a plate and go back to the living room.

I set the tray down on the coffee table. I stand there with my mouth open. Our Christmas tree is completely decorated.

"Six. How did you do that? I've only been gone ten minutes."

"Must be Christmas magic, the kind you don't believe in."

"Oh, come on. Who's here? Come on out. Where're you hiding?" I ask, looking behind the sofa. I'm sure he must have had help.

"Nice trick," I add, peering around the corner into the en-trance hall.

There's no one there.

Six adds two logs to the fire and moves the coffee table closer. He invites me to sit beside him on the *banco*, with the best view of the Christmas tree. I reach for one of the gingerbread cookies.

"No, not yet," he says, slapping my hand. "Those are for Santa. He's not going to come if you're naughty," he tells me.

"But I wasn't being naughty. I was being nice. I like ginger-bread."

We toast one another—me in Spanish, Six in Norwegian—with our mugs of *glögg*. Then he leans over and gives me a sticky-sweet kiss. I put my tongue in his mouth for a second taste.

"Well, in that case..." he remarks, taking another sip and giving me another kiss.

I have the feeling we could lie down on the floor in front of the fire and make love then and there.

"Let's have an early supper tonight," Six suggests. "What do you say? We could go to bed early, too, and snuggle up."

"Sure," I reply. "That sounds nice. I wouldn't mind settling in for a long winter's nap. I'm getting sleepy already. How much alcohol is in your *glögg*, Six?"

"It's mostly alcohol, Hypatia: red wine, port, rum, and brandy—plus the almonds, raisins, cloves, and cinnamon."

I feel snug and cozy sitting next to him—and a little horny, too. Putting my hand on his thigh, I take another sip of *glögg*. The fire and the mulled wine are keeping me warm inside and out. I lean into Six's shoulder for another mulled kiss.

Succumbing to the spell of Six's Christmas tree, I admit how beautiful it is: the best-decorated one yet. Maybe it has something to do with the unusual antique lights he found in the barn. I've begun to warm to the old hand-carved crèche from his father, too. It no longer looks so primitive. Instead, it seems abstract—a style I really like.

The evergreen is trimmed with every ornament from the tattered cardboard "Xmas" boxes. The cheerful lights are perfectly arranged. Six has festooned the tree with old-fashioned lead tinsel, too, a single strand at the end of each branch.

"Care for a little more *glögg* before I make supper?" he asks.

"Yes, please."

He goes out to the kitchen with the tray. I hear much clanging and banging. He returns with the two small mugs of hot spiced wine and a single broken gingerbread cookie on the plate.

"Your luck," he says. "I dropped it."

"You give *me* the busted cookie. I like that."

"I couldn't very well give a broken gingerbread man to Santa Claus, could I?"

"No, I suppose not," I reply, trying to look miffed. "That's one of the things I love most about you, Six: you are so innocent, so boyish. So *cute*," I add, breaking into a smile.

"That's better," he says, leaning towards me and puckering his lips. "Kisses sweeter than *glögg*," he sings.

"Doesn't have quite the same *ring*, does it, Six?" I remark, hoping he picks up on my emphasis.

"Want to give me a hand with supper? It's almost ready," he asks.

"I'm comfy right where I am, love. Our kitchen is too small for two cooks at a time."

I settle back and take a sip of *glögg*. Things would be perfect if only there were a tiny package beneath the Christmas tree, one too small to be anything else. I shut my eyes for a moment, picturing what it will look like on my finger.

———————⊃●⊂———————

I awaken when Six presses his lips against my cheek.

"There you are," he says, smiling. "I see you've finished your *glögg*."

"No, I haven't," I tell him. "There was lots left in my mug before I dozed off. The fire must have evaporated it all."

"Uh, huh," he remarks. "Or maybe Santa Claus got thirsty."

Six offers his hand to me and helps me up from the *banco*. I'm a little unsteady. Must have been the almonds and the raisins.

We go into the kitchen. It is warm and steamy and filled with aromas that make my mouth water in anticipation. I sit down at the table. There is a centerpiece of evergreen branches and a thick red candle. He busies himself at the stove and sink.

Six brings supper to the table. There is breaded whitefish, mashed peas, and bacon—in addition to the requisite *lutefisk* and boiled potatoes. The table looks very festive. I feel so snug.

Six lights the candle. We bow our heads for a silent grace. I dig in like a starving beggar.

"I'm glad to see you're hungry, Hypatia. Don't forget the pickled fish."

"Don't worry. I haven't forgotten about the *lutefisk*. Maybe I'll have some for dessert."

Six laughs, lingonberry sauce dripping from a corner of his mouth. I want to lick it off for him.

"The table looks very Christmasy, Six," I tell him.

"Thank you," he says. "Do you know how the colors of Christmas came to be red and green and white?"

"No, but I bet you do," I reply, taking another piece of whitefish and another helping of potatoes. I slather them with butter.

"The first Christmas trees had no lights or ornaments or tinsel. They were decorated with apples, the only fresh fruit that lasted into winter. The green was from the fir tree and the white, the snow that fell on its branches."

"How interesting," I tell him, taking another bite.

I am ravenous. I'm glad Six made enough tonight for all three of us. I'm waiting until bedtime to tell him I am *embarazada*, with child—his child.

While Six clears the table and washes dishes, I hastily wrap his present in the bedroom, retrieving it from beneath the bed. It is a blanket-lined denim jacket to replace his old one which is worn and faded. It's his favorite kind of winter jacket.

I get the package tucked beneath the tree. I notice there is no small package of the appropriate size competing for space on the knitted tree skirt his mother made. He walks in humming a Christmas carol. I'm not sure which one.

"I see Santa—or one of his helpers, more likely—has been here already. I didn't hear anyone come in, did you, Hypatia?" he asks.

His question makes me smile. His boyish dimples make me fall in love with him all over again

"My family's Mexican custom is to open presents on Christmas Eve," I remind him, hoping I can wheedle him into giving me my present tonight.

"My family's custom is to open gifts on Christmas Day," he replies. "We'll have to find a compromise, Hypatia. How about we open our gifts at the stroke of midnight?"

"Fair enough," I say.

Six proposes one more mug of *glögg*.

"Just one," I tell him. "I've got to stay awake until midnight."

He goes out to the kitchen. I drift away in thought watching the fire and the crackling embers and the twinkling Christmas tree.

Six returns with the tray of *glögg* and two gingerbread men.

"What about Santa?" I ask.

"Those *are* for Santa. I have something else in mind for *our* dessert."

"I couldn't eat another thing, Six. I'm stuffed."

"This dessert is non-fattening. In fact, it has negative calories."

"No such thing," I tell him.

"You wait and see," he replies, grinning.

Six places two smaller logs on the fire. We snuggle up next to each other and sip our warm *glögg*. I could not be more content and cozy.

It is nearly eleven o'clock: only an hour to go until we open our presents. Six leads me by the hand.

"Dessert in the bedroom?" I ask. "Sounds kind of kinky."

"That all depends," he says, smiling at me with his dimples on their high-beams.

Six pulls off his sweater and longjohn shirt and reaches for the buttons of his Levi's.

"Hurry up, Hypatia. Your dessert is getting cold."

It takes me three seconds to realize what he's talking about, but first, I have to pee.

Returning to the bedroom, I get undressed as quickly as I can. I wonder when the baby will begin to show and if anything I have to wear will fit.

Six is already beneath the quilt and covers, doing his best to warm the sheets on my side of the bed. He's such a sweet man.

He is tenting the sheet when I crawl in beside him. I put one leg over his legs and stroke his middle leg with my fingers.

He rolls over on me and pushes his erection between my legs, rubbing it between my thighs. It's getting me plenty excited.

Then Six grabs hold of my shoulders and pulls me over on top of him. It feels as though we are wrestling. I sit up, straddling him, and pull the covers around my shoulders to keep warm. The bedroom is the coldest room in the house—though we're doing our best to remedy that.

Positioning myself over him, I ease myself down and take his hard-on into me a little at a time. Gently bouncing up and down on my knees, I enjoy the sensation, slowing down when I must to prolong our love-making. I watch his eyes for signs.

Six's face shines; his ice-blue eyes register a glint of fire.

We join hands, our fingers intertwined, and rock back and forth, slow or fast, walking our love-making back from the edge of climax, trying to make it last. We have gone from wrestling to acrobatics. I am breathless.

When, finally, I feel him throb and spurt inside me, I come, too, shivering from the electricity of my orgasm. Leaning forward, I lie down on top of Six. We kiss until his hard-on diminishes and he withdraws.

"Merry Christmas," he says. "I'm pretty sure that was the best ever, but maybe we'll have to try it couple more times to be sure."

The gonging clock he inherited from his grandmother strikes midnight. I roll away from him and scramble from beneath the covers.

"Time to open presents," I announce, hastening naked into the living room to retrieve Six's present.

I awaken the fire with a couple of pokes and add another log. Holding my hastily-wrapped gift for Six against my breasts, I stand admiring our beautiful Christmas tree with the old red, white, and blue lights. Six hollers to me, asking what's taking me so long.

There was no present for me beneath the tree. I see no little package on my night-table or on his, either. I put Six's present on his chest and crawl back under the covers.

Six rubs his hands all over me to get me warm again. Propping his pillow behind him, he sits up in bed and tears the wrapping paper open. I set my pillow against the headboard, too, and watch his boyish delight at such an ordinary gift.

"Thank you, Hypatia," he tells me, leaning over to give me a kiss. "It's time to retire my old jacket except for work. My favorite, too—Levi's, with a Pendleton lining. What's this?" he asks, at last noticing the small card I placed in the pocket, leaving the button open on the flap so he'd find it.

I can read my note in his face as he peruses it. He reads it a second time. *Merry Christmas, Daddy.* He turns to me and, placing a hand behind my head, draws me to him for yet one more long kiss.

"The best present ever, Hypatia. I had my suspicions, though."

"Oh, you did, huh?"

"Yes," he replies, turning on his high-beams. "You've been eating like a trucker at the Sagebrush Diner. I told my buddy Antonio. He thought you might be pregnant."

"He spoiled my surprise," I say, pinching Six's butt.

"No, he didn't. All I had before your note were suspicions. Now I know. I've been thinking of names."

"Oh, you have, huh?"

"Yes, I have. What do you think of *José*?"

"My family would love a grandchild with a Spanish name. And they'd love *you* more than they do already. But what if it's a girl?"

"Then how about *Josefina*?"

"All right," I tell him. "I'm just happy you want to start a family."

"Well, it wasn't my decision alone, you know. I think you had something to do with it, too."

"I guess so, Six. I'm incredibly happy—for us and for the baby."

We find it hard to kiss when we are smiling.

"OK," I tell him. "It's time to model your new jacket for me."

"Now?"

"I want to see if it fits."

He crawls out of bed reluctantly and dons the stiff denim jacket wearing nothing else. The sheets are still warm where he has lain.

Six looks like some mythical creature—half man and half blue beast. I make him turn around so I can see the back. He's gotten me horny all over again.

"Well?" he asks.

"It looks good to me," I reply, "but maybe that's because you're in it. Come back to bed, Six."

He leaves his new jacket on. I grab the sheet and the quilt and raise them up for him to crawl back in. I feel something slightly sharp beneath his pillow.

"What's this?" I ask, retrieving the offending object.

"Merry Christmas, Hypatia," he says.

It is a box of just the right size. I tear the gaudy green ribbon and bright red Christmas paper off like an impatient child. There is no ring. I unfold a tiny note.

Hypatia, will you marry me?

"My God, Six. Yes, I will marry you. Most definitely, *Yes*."

Six unfolds his hand. A ring rests in his palm, gold with three small diamonds.

"My ring. My engagement ring. I'd about given up hope. Thank you, Six. *You* have to put it on my finger," I tell him, holding up my hand.

"But I didn't get you the ring, Hypatia. It must have been Santa Claus."

"Sure it was," I tell him, making no attempt to conceal the sarcasm in my voice.

"I'm glad you're finally coming around to believe in the spirit of Christmas."

He's so old-fashioned, so traditional. I expect him to slip out of bed again to propose to me on bended knee, naked except for his new jacket.

He slips the ring on my finger and leans over to kiss me. He's right. This is the best Christmas ever.

The ring's many facets catch the sparkling lights from the Christmas tree and the glowing embers from the hearth. I can't quite explain the strange optics to myself. The living room is opposite the kitchen, not the bedroom. Six notices the reflected and refracted red, white, and blue lights, too.

"Must be magic," he says, shrugging his shoulders.

I turn the ring around on my finger several times and hold my hand at different angles to admire it. The tiny diamonds scatters the tricolor Christmas lights all around the room. Six seems fascinated by the effect, too.

"Christmas is a magical time of year, Hypatia. Nearly everyone agrees. It must be Christmas magic—the kind you don't believe in."

I want to contradict him, but I'm not so convinced I'm right. I ask him again about the old-fashioned lights on the tree and how it's possible none of the bulbs has burned out in all this time, how they're all still shining brightly. He shrugs, and turns on his most boyish, elfish grin.

"I don't think it has much to do with electricity, Hypatia. *Oldefar* and his friend Edward have been dead for a long time. Think of all the people—grown-ups and children—that those lights have brought joy and pleasure to during all those years. They're still working because their magic is still working. That's my guess."

Unable to come up with a better explanation on the spot, I nod my head, agreeing with him.

Six takes off his new jacket and we nestle down under the covers, snuggling closer. Six yawns and slips slowly down into sleep. I can tell by his breathing.

Though my hand is cold outside the quilt, I want to look at the ring and its sparkling flashes of red, white, and blue for the rest of the night.

I scoot closer to my boyfriend, my soon-to-be husband. I feel more festive than I ever have before. In a strange way, it seems like my very *first* Christmas.

THE CHRISTMAS PACKAGE

A week before Christmas, a package arrived. We sat at the kitchen table slurping our chicken noodle soup, my sister Ethel and I and our mother. The rap on our kitchen door scared what my mother calls "the bejesus" out of us.

"You girls finish your lunch. You don't want to be late getting back to school. I'll see who it is."

Ethel is five minutes older than me, but sometimes she doesn't act like she's twelve years old. She's so immature. We re not quite identical, either. Her brown hair and eyes are lighter than mine. I think I'm prettier.

It is Miss Philomena Squidge, the postmistress. She has parked her tiny postal van with the steering wheel on the wrong side in our driveway. All U.S. postal delivery trucks have the steering wheel on the right side so the mailman can reach into mailboxes. My mother said in England everybody, except for drunk drivers, drives on the wrong side of the road. It must be scary.

"You have to sign for it," Miss Squidge says. "It's sure come a long way."

"Where's it from?" our mother asks.

"I don't know. I can't make it out. Well. Gotta run. It's the time of year I start getting real bunched up."

"Thank you," our mother tells her, opening the back door for the postmistress.

Ethel and I go back to our lunch. Mama turns the package over and around and back again trying to figure out who sent it.

There are stamps and stickers and labels from all over the world pasted across every square inch. Only here and there does a scrap of the original brown parcel paper show through.

"Do you know why butcher's paper is brown?" Ethel asks.

"Why don't you ask me if I'm even a little bit curious," I tell her.

"Caroline, be nice or Santa won't visit you. The Krampus will come in his place," my mother warns. "Please, tell us, Ethel. We're eager to know why brown paper is brown."

"Because," Ethel says, wagging her head from side to side and smirking at me, "they used to use the linen wrappings from mummies for making paper. But the tannin and bitumen and nasty parts of the mummies stained the paper brown. They couldn't use it for printing so they sold it to butcher's to wrap their meat in."

"Ewww," I tell my sister. "That's disgusting. I'm becoming a vegetarian."

"Finish your soup, Caroline."

"What about the package?" Ethel asks.

"We'll peek into it together after school, before Dad and Tony get home."

I make a point of taking every last piece of chicken out of my soup, leaving the chunks beside my bowl for my sister to see how she's ruined my appetite.

Ethel gets to the kitchen door before me. Mom sits at the kitchen table much as we left her, still trying to figure out the parcel from the mysterious sender.

"I wrote down everything from the package even if I didn't know what it meant or even what language it was in," Mom tells us. "Just in case it gets ripped opening it, as I'm sure it will."

Our mother shows us the pages of notes she's taken on the things written on all six sides of the box. She's filled about a dozen pages with writing and sketches.

"I'll untie the knot and you girls can spool up the twine. It's good, sturdy twine."

There's enough string to wrap four packages. Our mother uses all her skills as a former Cub Scout Den Mother for our brother Tony's den to undo the knot. She gives up in frustration. Ethel hands her the kitchen shears.

"Thank you, dear. Did I ask for them? I don't remember."

"It's the Gordian solution, Mama. When King Gordius faced an impossible knot, he withdrew his sword and sliced right through it."

"Where'd you hear that one, Ethel?" I ask my sister.

"World History class."

"I'm in the same period. Where was I when Mr. Sanford delivered that gem?"

"Asleep, probably," she says, twisting her mouth into a smirk.

I want to astound everyone with a witty comeback, but nothing comes to mind. I punch Ethel's arm instead—the last word in unwinnable arguments.

"Girls. Stop that. Roll up the twine onto this ball of it. Nice and tight. I don't want the ball coming undone."

I unwind the heavy brown string from the package and feed it to my sister, who wraps it around the growing ball of twine. Then we switch tasks.

The ball of string is getting big. It just keeps coming. At last we reach the end. I cut the twine—Ethel's Gordian solution to knotty problems. Mother attaches the end to the ball with a large tack and puts it back in the pantry.

Mama suggests unwrapping the package slowly so we do not damage any fancy Christmas wrapping paper on the actual present inside.

"How would she know there's Christmas paper inside?" I whisper in Ethel's ear.

We grab opposite ends of the package and rip the brown postal paper to shreds in under five seconds. Our mother sucks in her breath in horror—and then expels it in gusts of laughter.

"That's one way to do it," Mama says.

The wrapping paper on the actual gift depicts holly sprigs and berries, pine boughs and pine-cones, all of it sprinkled with snow. Each of us must touch it to convince ourselves the present is not really wrapped in holly and pine sprigs and fresh snow.

Our father, followed by our fifteen-year-old brother, Tony, and a blast of wind, burst into the kitchen. Papa looks around. Tony warms his hands by the woodstove. He looks more like Dad, black hair and blue eyes.

"What's going on here?" our father asks.

"A package arrived, dear—addressed to the entire Young family," Mama says, giving him a kiss. "The girls just took off the twine and the brown parcel paper. They applied a little Christmas enthusiasm. Right, girls?"

My sister and I nod. I hate it when we do the same things at the same time.

"Isn't this pretty paper, Papa?" Ethel remarks.

Our father, too, touches the festively-wrapped package.

"Very realistic. Fooled me," he says.

Tony turns around from the stove long enough to run his fingers across the package. He raises his eyebrows. My brother uses no more words than he has to. Still, it does not make up for Ethel's surfeit of words. I can't wait to use that word in a sentence.

"Are you all right, Tony?" our mother asks. "You're shivering."

My brother shrugs.

"He got chilled, Delia," my father says. "We got rained and snowed on—but we got the truck started. I'm sorry he had to miss school."

"I'll bet Tony wasn't sorry," my sister remarks.

Tony shakes his head. Everyone does his talking for him. It's quite a racket he's got going. I get so tired of explaining myself. Maybe my brother can teach me his trick some time.

———◦———

After the supper dishes are washed and put away, our mother brings out the package wrapped in Christmas paper again. Tony looks as bored as it's possible for a teenager to look without taking his eyes off the package for even a second. His feigned lack of interest doesn't fool me, even if he's not trying to fool me.

"What's this note say?" Papa asks.

"What note?" my sister and I and our mother ask all at once.

Tony cranes his neck to have a better look.

"It's Finnish," he says.

"Sure it is," I say, putting on Ethel's most sarcastic smirk.

"The language of Santa Claus," Ethel remarks.

"If only there *was* a Santa Claus," I shoot back.

"I can assure you there is," Tony pipes in.

"Children," our father says. "'Tis the season. Not a time for squabbles. How do you come by a knowledge of Finnish, son?"

"A project in our geography class," he replies, "to write a pen-pal in another country. I got assigned to this girl in Finland. She already knew a lot of English so she taught me Finnish instead. It says, 'Do not open until Christmas.'"

"Not fair," Ethel and I screech. "Not fair."

Our father holds his ears and looks at us sternly.

"Are you sure, Tony?" he asks.

"I'm sure, Pop. *Do not open until Christmas.*"

Our sighs of disappointment—all of us—are nearly enough to extinguish the big red Christmas candle on the buffet.

"Christmas is only a week away," my father reminds us. "I'll set the package up here on the sideboard for now. Tomorrow, Tony can go with me to the woods to cut down the second nicest tree we find."

"Why not the nicest, dear?" our mother asks.

"I always leave that one for Santa to give to a family less fortunate."

"That's very much in the spirit of Christmas," our mother says. "I approve. You dress warmer tomorrow, Tony. Layers. Longjohns. I don't want you getting sick for the holidays."

"Me, neither," he says.

Our mother gives the package a little pat—sort of a caress—and smiles. Papa turns out the light. We say good-night to each other and go to our rooms: Mom and Dad, me and Ethel, and Tony by himself. He's got it made. Though it's a couple years off, I can't wait until he moves out and I get his room—well, if he goes to college, that is. His room's not much bigger than our parents' closet.

No doubt the gears in all of our heads are turning overtime tonight, trying to figure out what could be in that package—and who might have sent it.

———◦———

The next morning, I get up before anyone. I go to the kitchen for a glass of water, passing the sideboard in the dining room. I knew it. The package is not there.

"It's gooone," I screech, drawing the word out like taffy. I say it again, louder and more shrill.

My father is the first on the scene: no shirt on, just his longjohns. Mom is not far behind, in her short nightgown. They are as wide-eyed as a pair of owls.

"What's the matter, dear?" my mother asks. "What happened?"

"It's g-g-gone," I say, stuttering. "The package is gone."

Tony sticks his tousled head out of his doorway and waves his arm in a gesture of dismissal. He closes his door again.

Last out of her royal cocoon is Princess Ethel, the prime suspect—at least I think she is. She wears her oversized sweatshirt. She's barefoot.

"It's in the living room, under the Christmas tree," she announces. "I actually got up *before* you, Caroline, but I went back to bed."

"What Christmas tree?" my dad asks. "We haven't got one yet. Tony," he shouts. "Come in here, Tony."

My brother arrives already in jeans and a T-shirt and mocassins.

"Nice tree," he says. "I thought I was going with you to look for one, Pop."

"You didn't bring this tree home?"

"Nope. Must've been Santa," Tony says.

"I guess you're right," our father tells him, "though he's pretty early this year."

"He's got a lot of stops, Dad. Maybe he wanted to get a

jump on things."

My brother and father smile at each other like there's a conspiracy afoot. Why are the men in the family so sappy about Christmas. They're like grown-up boys.

Our mother, of a more practical bent, pulls the package from beneath the gorgeous, perfectly formed evergreen. I don't care how it got here. It's the best tree we ever had.

"This is not the same package," Mama announces. "This one's taller and not as wide."

"I think you're right, Delia," my father tells her. "This package is deeper."

"And not quite as long," Ethel says.

"I think it's definitely larger," I chime in.

"Well, it's the same Christmas paper as before," Tony says.

We all nod, happy, I think, that we agree on something. Tony has that knack of a peacemaker. I will miss him when he moves out.

Mom announces she will make us all a big breakfast. My sister pitches in to help, angling for some favor, no doubt. Dad asks Tony for help getting the lights and Christmas decorations down from the garage rafters and up from the cellar. Tony waits for Dad to get dressed. We're the last two in the living room.

"You bought the Christmas tree, right?" I ask Tony. "You and Dad are pulling a prank."

"No, Sis. I had nothing to do with the tree. Pretty sure Dad didn't, either. I honestly believe Santa brought it. That's the only explanation that makes sense."

"Maybe to you," I reply, "but not to me. The package came from a real person, too."

Tony puts on his sly smile. I decide to change the subject—at least a little.

"What do you wish for, Tony? What do you hope is in the mystery package?"

"I'd really like to visit Inge in Finland next summer—you know, get to know her and stuff. So, it'd be cool if there were an airline ticket somewhere in that box."

"I wish I had enough money to get Mom enrolled in the

ceramics class she'd like to take," I say.

I lean into Tony's shoulder and whisper. "And while I'm just wishing—since it doesn't cost anything—I'd arrange for Dad to go on the hunting trip to Skyhigh Lodge he's been eager to take with his buddies."

"Maybe if we pooled our money," Tony suggests, "and Ethel kicked in her portion, we'd be able to get both Mom and Dad what they've got their hearts set on."

"Get real, Tony. Do you have any idea what ceramics classes and hunting trips cost?"

"I wasn't saying we'd be able to afford what they want. I was just imagining that the mystery package might just have something in it for each of us. Didn't Mom say it was addressed to the Young *family*?"

"Go ahead. Keep dreaming," I tell him. "We don't even know who sent it."

"Santa Claus, of course."

"You're impossible, Tony."

Our dad comes in wearing his weekend clothes of faded jeans and his favorite threadbare sweatshirt.

"Who's impossible?" he asks.

"Tony thinks there's something in the mystery Christmas package for each of us: whatever we've most set our hearts on."

"All in one little box? Well, maybe. Santa does some neat stuff when no one's looking."

"You're both impossible, still believing in Santa Claus."

My dad and brother stand looking at me with stunned expressions, as though I'd hurt their feelings. I bypass the kitchen, where there seems to be a serious mother-daughter conversation taking place between Ethel and Mom, and go up to my room.

I'm not sure my dad and Tony really believe in Santa Claus. They're probably saying they believe in him just to annoy me. Well, it worked.

Counting the money in my little wooden box, I come to the same sum I did in the twenty previous tallies. $1.87 is not going to buy anyone's dreams, especially those who count on Santa bringing them what they most want.

I wish I had enough for everyone's dream. I'd like to get Ethel the astronomy book she's got her heart set on, but it's very expensive. Then I ask myself, *What normal twelve-year-old wants to be an astronomer when she grows up?* My sister does, but she's hardly normal.

I pick out what I'm going to wear and push my dresser drawer shut. I choose a red skirt, white blouse, and a green sweater. I'm feeling very Christmasy.

When I come downstairs, the living room looks like a dump: cardboard and paper scattered everywhere. My father, without benefit of a step-stool, hangs an oversized, glittery silver ornament near the top of the Christmas tree. Ethel and my mom, both still in their bathrobes and fuzzy slippers, point this way and that, directing where to hang the ornament. They are like a pair of backseat drivers offering advice in stereo.

Once he helped Dad excavate the boxes of lights and decorations, Tony cleared out. I should have followed his lead.

"Don't be ridiculous," I say. "That ornament is too big for so high up on the tree. Switch it with that smaller one there, near the bottom."

My father, still holding the big silver ball, turns around and raises his eyebrows.

"Well?" he asks the decorating experts on the sofa.

"Maybe she has a point, Jim," my mother says.

"The only point she has is at the top of her head," Ethel remarks, sticking her tongue out at me.

She's the most immature twelve year-old I know, beating every boy at school in juvenile behavior. I decide to go up to Tony's room and see how he's making out.

"Knock, knock," I say.

"It's not locked," he replies.

Tony's room is even more of a disaster zone than the living room. His clothes and shoes, and a mix of books and papers, sketches and music albums, have been tossed through a wind tunnel and flung around the room.

"Come on in, Sis," he says, giving the corner of the blanket on his unmade bed a flip, clearing a space for me to sit. "Watch your step."

Tony sits down on his window sill, the last unoccupied space in his room.

"I liked our conversation before," my brother says. "We should do it more often. But I forgot to ask you what *you* hope is in the Christmas package."

His kindness stuns me. It always does. Teenagers are not supposed to consider the feelings of others, especially a kid sister's.

"I thought I might like to have this pendant I saw with a small stone of polished turquoise, but I'm really not expecting anything this Christmas."

"If that's what you expect," he advises, "that's exactly what you'll get. Dream big, Caroline. Spare no expense of thought."

I laugh at his turn of phrase.

"I think the mystery package is a prank. The whole business of Christmas is phony," I tell him, hoping it won't hurt his feelings.

"Sure it is," he replies. "But there's something at its heart, under all the sparkles and glitter, that is real. I think it is our better selves hiding inside."

"Then that's what I want to wish for us for Christmas," I tell him. "Better selves for everyone."

Tony laughs. "That's a pretty tall order, Sis. Think Santa will be able to deliver the goods?"

"If he's more than a figment of your imagination, he will."

"Santa's real," Tony tells me. "Maybe not quite as substantial as you and me, but he does things no one can quite explain."

"Such as?" I reply.

At that instant, an avalanche of books and T-shirts—and even the core of an apple and a pizza rind—crashes from his night table to the floor.

"That pile has been teetering for a while," he says, chuckling. "Maybe you could help me clean up this mess sometime—

before Christmas, maybe."

"Sure, Tony. No time like the present. What do you say?"

"It beats getting involved in discussions over how to hang the Christmas lights."

"They've moved on from there. Now the squabbles are about where to hang the ornaments."

My brother and I go downstairs to fetch the kitchen trash can and the laundry basket.

Tony seems so pleased that I would help him clean his room.

"It'll sure make Mom happy," he tells me.

"I'm sure it will," I reply.

Maybe, I think, *my $1.87 will be more than enough to make everybody happy at Christmas.* So far, I haven't spent a nickel, and my brother is grinning from ear to ear.

The three days before Christmas pass with my sister and I poring over our mother's notebook with all the original words and markings on the mystery package's brown parcel paper.

Ethel and I don't agree on what most of the words are, but when we do, we make a note of it. There are so few hours remaining before the mystery Christmas package gives up its secrets that I do not want to get in an argument over it.

"I'm not sure," my sister says, "but I think that address is in Finland, a town in Finland. Why don't we ask Tony?"

"There's only one town in Finland as far as our brother is concerned, Ethel, the one where Inge lives."

"Then why don't we check Dad's atlas?" she suggests.

"OK," I say. "But not a word to anyone until we're sure. I don't want to look like a fool."

"It's too late for that," she says, doing her best to suppress her smile.

It is more like the teasing we used to do—before it got to be so serious. Maybe that's what it means to "remain as little children" at Christmas. Ethel and I had forgotten how to have fun.

"I liked it better when our teasing was funny," I tell Ethel.

"Me, too," she says. "I miss our goofing around."

We hug each other. I'd forgotten how much I like her.

Setting the world atlas on the coffee table, we look up the plate for Finland. It's a long country, so it takes up two pages. The name of the town is not in the index. Maybe it's too small.

Ethel and I each take a page to scrutinize. It's very tiring because none of the strange names mean anything to us. There's nothing close to the name of the town we're looking for.

Our mother enters the living room. Ethel closes the atlas. She and I look up.

"That's nice to see you girls cooperating," Mom says. "What are you looking up, if I may ask?"

"The name of one of the towns on the package. It might be where Santa Claus was born," Ethel tells our mother.

"I didn't know Santa was born," Mom says. "I thought he just always... *was*."

"The town where he was born is in Lapland, the most northern part of Finland," Ethel tells her. "The town is called Korvatunturi, but we couldn't find it on the map."

"Maybe Tony knows where it is," our mother suggests.

Ethel tells our Mom we'll ask our brother. I put Dad's heavy world atlas back on the bottom shelf. My sister and I go upstairs and knock on Tony's door. He says something that's not in English. Ethel and I look at one another.

"That was Finnish for 'Please. Come in,'" he says.

"We were wondering if you know where the town of Korvatunturi is."

"Sure. It's on the Arctic Circle. Legend has it that is where Santa Claus was born."

"I think Santa himself is a legend," I remark. "Is it anywhere close to where Inge lives?"

"She's a long way from Korvatunturi. Why? You thinking of going there?"

"No," Ethel says. "It's one of the addresses we could make out on the mystery package."

"Really? That's so cool. We got a present from *Joulupukki*."

"Who?" I ask.

"*Joulupukki.* That's what the Finns call Santa Claus. Literally, it means *The Christmas Goat.*"

"He does look kind of like an old goat, doesn't he?" I suggest.

We laugh together as we haven't in quite a while.

"Thanks, Tony," Ethel tells him. "We'll let you know if we decipher any more of Mom's notes."

My sister and I retreat to our room and lie down on our beds. She is now convinced the package is really from Santa. I am the last holdout for sanity.

———————⟨⟩———————

The door is open, so I knock on the doorframe to my parents' bedroom.

"Come in, Caroline," my mother says, hastily tucking something wrapped in Christmas paper beneath her pillow.

"Mom, can I borrow some money? Just until I get a job next summer. I want to get Ethel the astronomy book she's been yearning for."

"Next summer? How much is the book?"

"Ninety-nine dollars and ninety-nine cents. I have enough saved for the tax."

"What makes you think I have that kind of money? That's what one day at the Skyhigh Lodge would cost your dad, and I don't have money for that. I wish I could be Santa Claus and give everybody what they want."

She takes the change purse from her dresser drawer.

"I could loan you five dollars," she says.

"It's five dollars more than I had a few minutes ago," I tell her. "Things are looking up."

My mother and I laugh.

"It's very nice of you, Caroline, to want to be so generous to your sister. I'm happy you two are getting along better. I hope you'll find a way to get your sister that book. Have you asked Santa?"

"Mom," I say. "Are you serious?"

"Santa doesn't read minds, you know. You have to write

him. There's nice notepaper in the sideboard downstairs. I read somewhere that Santa is especially attentive to requests that do not come from the intended recipient of the gift."

"Thanks, Mom," I say.

I leave her bedroom. I take a sheet of the good note paper and an envelope from the sideboard. No one saw me.

The gears of my thoughts are turning madly, devising a way to trap Santa in a fabrication. If he's not real, he's just not going to answer my note. It's that simple. I'll have proof he's not real.

I feel rather proud of myself.

———————⊃◦⊂———————

At last Christmas Eve arrives. I thought it would never get here. I've left my note to Santa under the tree, at the back beneath the lowest branch where it is hidden from view.

The family sits down to our supper. There is much good-natured teasing and laughter during our meal. Despite the fact that Mom and Ethel prepared our favorite treats of family tradition, no one seems hungry. I'm guessing all any of us can think about is the package that arrived from Finland one week ago. We do not even wash the dishes but simply clear the table and stack the plates in the sink.

"Look," Mother says, pointing to the package under the tree.

It is now a cube about a foot square wrapped in paper with a pattern of huge silver snowflakes, one to each side. The snowflakes look as though they've been sculpted in ice. I consider the fact that the package substitution occurred while all of us sat around the supper table. *Who could it have been?* I wonder.

Dad picks the package up from under the tree and places it on the coffee table, sitting down next to Mom. We look around the room at each other, puzzled looks on each face.

The little tag on the box now reads, "Open at once."

I share the loveseat with Ethel. Tony makes himself cozy in the rocking chair next to the hearth. He stirs the embers and adds two logs.

"Thank you, Santa, for our family present," my father says.

"Merry Christmas."

There are splashes of water as the wrapping paper melts. By the time my father gets it unwrapped, nothing remains of the festive paper but a puddle. I see his hands tremble as he opens the plain brown cardboard box. We all stand up to peer down into it.

Beneath a mound of wrinkled brown paper packing, is Ethel's astronomy book. There's nothing else in the box. I am happy for my sister, but a bit disappointed that Mom and Dad and Tony have received nothing.

Ethel smiles from ear to ear as four pairs of eyes stare at her.

"What's this?" she asks. "Bookmarks?"

She turns to one of the bookmarks and begins reading the page.

"Oh," she says. "I guess this is for you, Dad."

She hands him the envelope with his name on it. We impatiently urge him to rip it open.

"Oh, my God," he says. "A week's stay at the Skyhigh Lodge—room, meals, and hunting guides included. Delia, it's very nice, but you shouldn't have."

"I didn't," Mom replies.

Dad looks around the room, searching for the Christmas culprit. Dad kisses Mom.

"Here's another one of the bookmarks. This one's for you, Mom," Ethel says, taking out the envelope and handing it to her.

We watch her intently. Tears form in her eyes. She leans towards Dad and gives him a big smooch.

"My ceramics class," Mom announces. "Full tuition and all supplies. I don't know what to say."

"It wasn't me, Delia," Dad tells her. "I wanted to get you enrolled in that class, but I didn't get all the overtime I'd hoped for. Honest. It wasn't me."

Next comes a long, narrow envelope for Tony.

"No," he says. "It can't be. Impossible."

He waves the paper slips at us. We lean towards him to have a better look.

"What is it, Tony?" Mom asks him.

My brother is choked up. He has trouble getting the words out.

"Air fare to Finland," he says. "Round-trip, aboard Täelfinn, the national airline."

Our mother gets up and gives Tony a hug and a kiss.

"I'm so happy for you. You must be thrilled."

"I am, Mama. I am. How did you guys do it?"

"It wasn't us, Tony," Dad tells him. "This was going to be a very lean Christmas."

Tony gets up and races around the living room, waving and flapping the airline ticket. His feet barely touch the floor once.

When Tony settles down, our father asks whether there isn't an envelope for me in Ethel's astronomy book. Ethel adjusts the heavy tome on her lap and flips through the pages. An envelope flutters to the carpet.

It looks like the note I'd left for Santa beneath the tree. The envelope is still sealed. The name "Santa" is crossed out and "Caroline" written beneath it. I tear it open, a bit nervous with all eyes upon me.

A turquoise pendant on a fine silver chain falls into my lap. On the side of the tiny card, opposite my note to Santa, is written, in a different color ink:

Dear Caroline,

Your mother was right, dear child, as mothers often are. I do pay special attention to requests for people that come from someone else, someone who loves them. That showed me you know the real meaning of Christmas. God bless you.

Santa Claus
(The Old Goat)

I had put all the money I had in the world, all $1.87, and the five dollars from Mom, in the envelope before I licked the flap and left it behind the tree. I wanted to do my part. My money was now gone, but the five dollars I borrowed from Mom was still there. Ethel had her book, Mom her class, Dad his trip, and Tony his ticket. And I had my turquoise pendant.

The impossibility of it all makes me smile. We each thought some other member of the family was responsible for our Christmas magic. I, of course, knew it could only have been Santa Claus.

"Something has made you happy, Caroline," my mother says.

"Yes," I reply. "Very happy. *Hyvää joulua, Joulupukki.* Merry Christmas, Santa."

Tony chuckles.

We are on our way to having our best Christmas ever—all for only $1.87, cheap at twice the price.

A DOGGIE'S TALE

I saw the young dog nearly every day on the way home after school. He was always tied up in his grassless yard when I went past. He was growing up fast.

Trying to describe the mutt to my best friend at school, whose name is José, I realized I hadn't paid very close attention to what the dog looked like. I saw mostly his eyes: "big as dinner plates," as my grandma would say, and deep as wells. He looked sad. The dog came to me as close as he could. His leash, hooked to a metal stake in the ground, didn't let him come all the way to the tall wire mesh fence.

The doggie was sort of shaggy, but also kind of wire-haired. His ears stood straight up and pointy sometimes and were floppy at others. Some days he seemed like a small breed of grown-up dog and on others a large puppy who had not outgrown his playfulness. The one thing I was certain of was the color of his dull coat: reddish-brown, like the dirt he was so fond of digging up in his yard.

I decided the dog was what my dad called a "Heinz," like the ketchup. He was a combination of fifty-seven kinds of dog. The poor doggie had no one to play with and hadn't even a ball or a bone to amuse himself with. There was never a food or water bowl in the yard or on the front doorstep. He had no doghouse to provide him shelter when it rained or snowed. I felt sorry for him.

One day, I brought him a cardboard box from behind the liquor store that he'd fit in. I tossed it over the fence as close to the house as I could pitch it. He knew exactly what it was for. He shook himself off in a spray of rainwater and crawled inside his new home. Turning around inside the box, he looked out and watched me. I huddled inside my poncho and hurried home.

Over the weekend, I decided the dog deserved to have a name, but I couldn't think of one that seemed right for him. They were either too long or too hard to pronounce in a hurry—like when I would need to call him home. Maybe I should ask the dog if he already has a name.

On Monday after school, I see the wet snow has collapsed his cardboard doghouse into a soggy mess. The dog comes toward me, to the end of his leash, wagging his tail, his tongue dangling. He looks skinny. I wish I had a treat to toss him. I'll save something for him from my supper tonight.

I think of climbing over the tall wire-mesh fence, but the spaces between the wires are too small for me to get my Keds into. Besides, the dog has trampled his yard into a muddy mess in the shape of a perfect circle because he's tied to the stake. I'd get dirty and get in trouble.

"Hi, boy," I say.

He stands at attention and pants faster.

"I don't know what to call you. I want to give you a name, but not if you've already got one," I tell him. "My name's Tony."

He barks once and gives a quick growl. It kind of sounds like my name.

"Do you have a name?" I ask.

He lets out another combination bark and growl.

"Did you say *Otto*?"

That was not one of the names I'd considered. He probably just said *Arf, Arf*, but he looks like an Otto. The name fits him. He bobs his head up and down and wags his tail from side to side. I take it as a *Yes*. I guess his name is Otto.

"I wish I could pet you."

Otto tugs hard on his leash, pulling the anchor out of the soggy ground. He bounds up to the fence, dragging the anchor behind him. He splashes me with his muddy front paws as he puts them on the fence. It's way too tall for him to climb or jump over.

My hand just fits through the fence. I scratch under Otto's chin. He makes a noise like a doggie purring. It makes me laugh. When he jumps down, he puts his head up against the wires and I scratch behind his left ear. After he's had enough, he turns himself around and shows me his other ear.

"I've got to be going, Otto, but I'll see you tomorrow. Sleep well."

He puts his paws back up on the fence, as if to keep me from leaving, and watches me until I turn the corner at the end of the block.

———————◦◦———————

"What happened to you?" my mom asks, looking at the muddy splashes on my clothes. "Just don't track it through the house. Go downstairs and change. There are clean jeans and sneakers in the basket."

"Yes, Mom," I say.

When I was a little kid, I got in a lot of trouble getting my new snowsuit dirty when I helped Grandpa shovel coal into the coal hopper with my toy shovel and bucket. Grandpa got in even more trouble. Now we have an oil furnace.

I'm not sure how it happens, especially when I'm trying to stay clean, but dirt always seems to find me and practically jumps on me. I'm like Charlie Brown's friend Pigpen. At least my poncho kept my sweater and jacket clean.

I look around the basement for a place Otto might stay. There's the old coal shed. He could have his own little house inside our house when the weather was rainy or cold and snowy. Maybe my dad could help me put a door on the shed so Otto could have some privacy.

"Tony, what're you doing down there? Supper's almost ready," my mom hollers down the basement steps.

"I'll be right up, Mom," I say.

I'd forgotten about changing clothes when I was scouting

out places for Otto to live in our basement. Maybe my mom and dad won't even let me have a dog. I'll have to start working on them right away. Christmas is only a week away. I scramble out of my dirty stuff and into fresh jeans and gym shoes.

"That's better," Mom says. "But you didn't wash your face."

My dad, sitting at the kitchen table, turns to look at me. He laughs.

"I've heard of Tony the Tiger," he tells me, "but never Tony the Leopard. You've still got spots of mud on your face, kiddo."

I go into the bathroom to rub water on my face. Going back to the kitchen, I take my place. Dad says grace and I dig in.

Our supper is spaghetti with Mom's canned tomatoes from last summer's garden. The spices she uses make it taste like what you'd get at the Mondo Italiano restaurant in town—lots of garlic and basil. I gobble it up and ask for seconds.

I think for minute of saving some of my supper to give Otto through the fence tomorrow, but how do I sneak spaghetti in my pocket? I don't know if Otto even likes spaghetti.

"Dad?" I say. "What happens when nobody lives in a house, but there's a dog tied up in the yard?"

"Is that where you got so dirty today?" my mom asks.

"Yes," I reply. "Otto's yard is very muddy."

"How do you know his name, Tony?" my dad asks.

"He told me, Dad. I didn't want to give him a new name if he already had one."

"I see," my dad says, finishing his plate but turning down Mom's offer for seconds.

"It's not right to abandon a dog when you move away," he adds. "I'll call Animal Welfare tomorrow. Maybe they'll find Otto a home in time for Christmas."

"What about here with us?" I say, sputtering.

"Please, dear," Mom says. "Not with food in your mouth. It's impolite. Who would take care of Otto?"

"I would," I declare, jumping to my feet and raising my hand.

"Simmer down," Dad tells me.

"I'm afraid your record for taking care of pets is not very good, Tony. Both of your turtles died," Mom reminds me.

"But they were so lazy, Mom—and dumb. All they did was sleep on the rock. I changed the water every three days but never caught them swimming in it. Turtles are boring. All they do is sleep."

"Despite their lack of conversational skills, son," my dad tells me, "they were your duty to care for. I'm not sure you're ready for the responsibility of a dog, Tony."

"Please, Dad. If I don't take care of Otto like I'm supposed to, you can send him back to the Animal Welfare. I promise I will take great care of him. You'll see."

"Well, what if you fall down on the job and you don't brush him or feed him or walk him? Can your mom and I send you to the dog pound instead of Otto?"

"Dad," I say, chuckling "You'd miss me an awful lot."

"Maybe," he says, ruffling my hair. "Or maybe not."

We both laugh.

"You two," my mom remarks. "It's hard to tell which of you is the bigger kid."

Dad asks me if I remember the address of the empty house where Otto lives.

"No, I didn't look," I tell him. "But it's on Arroyo Road near the firehouse."

"I'll look into it when you get me the house number, Tony. You are excused."

I help my mom carry our plates to the sink. I rinse them and put them in the dishpan, adding soap and warm water. It doesn't hurt to butter Mom up, even if Dad has the last word on Otto. If only I could arrange for Dad to meet him. I'm sure he'd fall in love with Otto, too.

On my way home today, Otto is not in his yard. His leash and collar are at the end of his uprooted anchor. The windows and doors of the bungalow are boarded up with plywood. The address above the front door frame is 245. I repeat it a few times so I don't forget.

I go into the neighboring driveway to have a look into Otto's back yard. The rear porch is unpainted and rotting. It looks ready to collapse. I call Otto's name.

Otto comes bounding from beneath the leaning porch steps. *That* is his home. His water bowl sits beneath the downspout. It is full. His food bowl is empty.

"Here, boy. Come on, Otto," I say.

I reach into my jacket pocket for the treat I brought Otto. I roll up the slice of salami from my sandwich and poke the slice of lunchmeat through the wire fence. It is full of lint from my pocket. Otto doesn't mind. He swallows it in two bites.

"I'm working on getting you out of jail, Otto," I tell him, scratching beneath his chin. "I'm gonna tell my dad tonight where you live and he'll get you sprung from this joint, pal," I say, doing my best impression of Edward G. Robinson. "You're gonna come live with me."

Otto barks and wags his tail. He follows me along the fence to his front yard. I stand on the sidewalk and pet him one more time behind his right ear.

"I gotta remember your address, Otto. Do you know where you live?"

The reddish-brown mutt utters a combination of a yelp, a woof, and yowling bark.

"That's right, Otto: 2-4-5. You're a pretty smart doggie."

I thought talking dogs were not real except on the Ed Sullivan Show. I guess I was wrong. But I'm sure they're pretty rare. I wonder what else Otto can say.

That night, after supper, I tell my dad where Otto lives.

———————⊃○⊂———————

The next day, I bring Otto some of my previous night's supper and some of today's lunch. This time I wrapped it in wax paper, but it leaked into my pocket anyhow.

"One day closer to Christmas and one day closer to freedom," I tell him. "Only three more days."

"Woof YELP yip, BARK growl WOOF," Otto says, greeting me at the fence.

"That's right. December 25th. Like my dad always tells me, *You're smarter than you look*."

Otto chuckles. I like that he has a sense of humor about himself. There are too many sourpuss dogs in the world.

He gobbles up whatever I hand him through the wire mesh. Otto is careful of my hands and licks them clean when he's finished. He is a gentle dog—and so smart.

"See you tomorrow, Otto," I say. "It's my last day of school before Christmas. We're going to be great friends, you and I."

He woofs his approval. I hurry home, looking over my shoulder at Otto, his paws up on the fence, until I turn the corner.

———————⸎———————

I try to hold back, but I rush to my dad the instant he sets foot in the kitchen to ask what the Animal Welfare people said.

"Whoa, pardner," he tells me. "Let a workingman get his jacket off."

"Sorry, Dad."

"How 'bout my cap, too?"

"Sure," I say.

He washes his hands at the kitchen sink and takes a beer out of the fridge. He offers me a Coke.

We sit down at the kitchen table. Mom joins us with her cup of tea.

"The Animal Welfare folks drove past the place several times. They didn't find a dog. No evidence of one, either, they said. Did you give me the right address, Tony? 2-4-5 Arroyo Road?"

"Yes, Dad. That's the right address. But Otto lives under the back porch and he doesn't come for strangers—only me. That porch is gonna collapse and fall down on him if we don't rescue him real soon—like before Christmas."

"They told me that house is slated for demolition, son."

"How could they be so stupid?" I ask. "They've gotta look

under the back porch. They should've come with wire cutters to get inside his yard."

"I'm sorry, Tony. They gave it a go. I can't tell them how to go about doing their job. I don't like people bossing me around who aren't my boss, either. I'm sure they tried their best."

"They didn't try hard enough," I cry, getting up from the table. "Couldn't we use *your* wire-cutters to get through the fence, Dad. Will you help me?"

"Help you get into jail? That's trespassing, Tony, even if nobody lives there. We have to do this the right way. Do you understand?"

"Yes, Dad," I say, going upstairs to my room.

I intend to pout for the rest of the evening, excusing myself from supper because I don't feel good. But I'm pretty hungry and I've got to get something for Otto, too. His rescue is taking much longer than I expected.

I've got only one more idea for getting Otto out in time for Christmas. Well, two ideas, actually, but I don't think I'd get away with trying to hide my dad's wire cutters under my sweatshirt. If Dad caught me borrowing his tools without asking, it would destroy every hope of his letting Otto come to live with us.

———————◦◦———————

It is now the Saturday before Christmas—just two more days. There's no more school until next year. Mom and Dad announce at breakfast that they will be going to look for our Christmas tree and "other last-minute shopping."

My friend José was not in school yesterday. I wonder if he's OK or just faking in order to get another day tacked onto our Christmas vacation.

I tell my parents I'll be going over to my friend José's. They warn me to be polite at my friend's house and to be home for supper. I promise I will.

José's mom answers the door.

"I am sorry, Tony. It was kind of last-minute. José decided to go with his older brother Tomás to visit their grandparents in Mexico for Christmas. He left you this."

Mrs. Morales hands me an envelope with my name on it in José's handwriting.

"Feliz Navidad," she says.

"Merry Christmas," I reply.

José's mom closes the door. I put the letter in my back pocket.

Disappointed, I walk home slowly. José and I were going to pal around today. He was going to help me figure out how to rescue Otto. Now, I am on my own. Even my dad won't help. I'm afraid the bulldozers will demolish Otto's house on top of him.

I walk a different way to Otto's house. He approaches the fence as soon as I turn the corner. *Did he smell me coming or something*, I wonder.

"Howl YELP," he says.

"Hello to you, too," I tell him.

I scratch the dirt on my side of his fence with the heels and toes of my gym shoes. I look around to make sure no one is watching. Otto gets the idea and starts digging on his side right next to the wire mesh. The ground is pretty hard.

The movie that gave me the idea to help Otto dig a tunnel under the fence was *The Great Escape*. I'd have to help him from my side if we were going to get him out in time for his juicy Christmas bone. I give him the sausage link I saved from breakfast and some mashed peas from last night's supper. He gobbles them both up.

"BARK yelp, ARF yip."

"You're welcome, Otto. I'll be back tomorrow. I gotta borrow a shovel or something. Maybe it'll rain. That'd make digging a lot easier. Tomorrow's Christmas Eve, you know."

"GROWL bark yap?"

"Yes, the day I'm gonna get you out of there. You can trust me, Otto. I always keep my promises."

He puts his paws up on the fence for his chin scratch. Tomorrow we'll be on the same side of the fence if it's the last thing I do.

I stop on the way home to read the card from my friend

José. I tear open the envelope. He's drawn me a beautiful Christmas card with colored pencils. José is a pretty good artist.

Merry Christmas, Tony.

I will see you before the New Year gets here. Good luck with your parents and Otto. I look forward to meeting your new dog.

Your pal,
José

———————◦○◦———————

I am not able to leave the house today, Christmas Eve, until after lunch. I've got a thick slice of ham for Otto. I have to be home by three o'clock. It's not much time to arrange Otto's great escape.

My parents are busy decorating our Christmas tree. It fills the house with its piney smell. My father puts the angel at the top. He hangs and adjusts the lights while my mother puts the ornaments and icicles on the branches, hanging the tinsel one strand at a time.

"I'll save some ornaments for you to put on the tree, Tony," my mom says. "Don't be late. You might miss Santa."

"Don't worry. I won't be late," I reply, smiling at her. I don't still believe in Santa Claus, but I definitely believe in Christmas.

I leave the house in my oldest clothes. At least it waited until I'd gone a couple blocks before it started raining, otherwise my parents might have not have let me go outside. The weather is halfway between rain and slushy snow.

I take my mom's garden spade from the shed and hide it beneath my old gym sweatshirt with the hood. Though I forgot my gloves, I'm not going back for them. I put my hood up.

It worries me that the Animal Welfare people could not find Otto. So far, I'm the only one who's ever seen him. Am I imagining him because I want a doggie so bad? Am I going crazy already like Uncle Ernie who hears voices and sometimes sees angels? I'm not even twelve years old yet. I thought only old people went crazy.

Otto waits for me in his front yard. He looks real enough to me. Wagging his tail and barking, he leads me along the fence around to the back yard. We won't be seen from there. Otto sits proudly beside a hole he's started right next to the fence. His legs and chest are all muddy. The hole is filling with rain and slush.

The wire mesh goes pretty far into the ground, probably to keep Otto from digging his way out and escaping. I start digging on my side. It's going to be lot of work and take a lot of time with the small spade I've got. Otto barks and goes back to working the hole on his side, flinging mud everywhere.

Though I do my best to stay clean, it's useless. I break the dirt up with my mom's garden trowel. Kneeling down, I scoop the mud with my hands like Otto does. My hands are cold.

I put my hands in either my jeans pockets or my jacket pockets to warm them up. There used to be a pouch in my gray sweatshirt, but it ripped off a long time ago. There are holes in the knees of my jeans where my longjohns show through. They've gotten muddy, too. But those longjohns are too short on me now anyhow. My socks barely reach them.

I'm going to be in a lot of trouble, but it will be worth it rescuing my dog from certain death beneath a bulldozer. Besides, I get scolded almost the same whether I've gotten just a little bit dirty or a whole lot muddy. I follow Otto's example and decide I might as well have fun.

Otto has reached the bottom of the fence mesh, but the hole keeps filling with more mud. I lie down on the ground to scoop it out with the trowel. I'm glad my mom is not as particular about her tools as my dad is about his.

The wire mesh below ground is rusty. I bend and break pieces off with the spade. Otto barks.

"You're right," I tell him. "You'll be a free dog in no time."

He flings more mud with his furious digging, splashing me, too. I'm muddy top to bottom. I bend the fence mesh up as far as I can so Otto does not get caught on it or get cut by it. My fingers feel like they will be the next things to break off.

I stand up and put my hands under my armpits, the last clean place on me. Otto also decides to take a break and sits down on his haunches and watches. It doesn't look like we'll have to dig the hole much deeper for Otto to squeeze through. He's going to need a bath, too. Only his eyes and teeth are still clean. He smiles at me. I'm pretty sure he's having a good time.

"Bark yip HOWL," he says.

"You're right, Otto. Mud *is* fun. It's worth getting in trouble for getting muddy."

We go back to our digging. Otto tries crawling through the tunnel but gets stuck in the middle of it. I lie on my belly and, gently grabbing hold of his front legs, pull him the rest of the way through our tunnel.

He's free at last.

I get up from the ground and crouch down to pet him. Otto licks my face and pushes me backwards. He stands on my chest and licks me some more. I guess he doesn't mind the taste of mud.

"We'd better get going, boy. I don't what time it is."

Otto scampers around me, running in circles and leaping up. I dance around him, too. We leave muddy footprints and pawprints on the damp sidewalk. The sleet doesn't do much to clean us off.

"We did it, Otto. You're a free dog in a free country."

"Yip arf GROWL, yap yip ARF BOWwow," he repeats.

Otto walks right beside me and waits for me to say it's OK to cross the street. He's a really smart dog.

My mom, standing at the kitchen sink sees us come into the back yard. She throws up the sash.

"My God, Tony. Did you roll in the mud? You wait out there. Dad will come down and open the basement door. You get cleaned up down there."

"Yes, Mom," I say. She didn't say a word about Otto.

My new dog is no longer beside me. He is scrunched down beneath one of the evergreens in our back yard. No wonder Mom didn't see him.

"It's OK, Otto. This is where I live. That was Mom."

I'm getting cold. The mud has soaked through to my underwear. My dad opens the basement door and waves me inside. He seems more amused than angry.

"It looks like you had fun," he says. "Where's the doggie you went to so much trouble to rescue?"

I look for Otto, but he's no longer beneath the evergreen. I go around the corner of the house to call him. He does not answer. My dad must have spooked him.

"He was just here, Dad," I tell him. "But Otto's a little skittish."

"Well, get in here, Tony. You don't want to get a cold for Christmas."

I go down the basement steps and dad closes the door. I'm worried about Otto.

"You strip out of your muddy clothes and throw them in the washtub. I'll bring you some soap and a washcloth."

My dad goes upstairs. I put the stopper in one side of the washtub and begin filling it from the hose.

I open the outside door and call to Otto. He appears at the top of the steps and shakes himself. He looks like the spinning brushes at the carwash. Muddy water sprays everywhere. Otto looks much better.

He slinks down the steps, tail wagging, but he does not come inside. My dad comes downstairs with soap and a washcloth.

"What're you doing with the door open?" he asks.

"I was letting Otto in. I'm going to give him a bath, too."

"There's no one there, son. Look," he says, shutting the basement door again.

Otto has disappeared.

"Come on, Tony. Get out of your muddy clothes. Want me to hold the hose on you?"

"No, it's all right," I tell Dad. "I'm worried about Otto. He followed me all the way home and then won't come inside."

"He probably has to get used to things," my dad says.

I untie my gym shoes and take off my blue jeans that are no longer blue. I unzip my jacket and my dad helps me out of my soaked sweatshirt and T-shirt. I put my muddy stuff in the wash-tub full of water. I am down to my socks and longjohns. I doubt they will ever be white again.

"Your mother says there's clean stuff in one of the laundry baskets. Don't dawdle now. Supper will be ready soon. If the weather's not too miserable, Tony, we'll go look for Otto after supper," my dad tells me.

"Thanks, Dad," I say.

My dad goes back upstairs. I open the back door, shivering. It is snowing.

Otto bounds down the steps and jumps right into the other washtub. I close the back door.

I put the rubber stopper in Otto's tub and put the hose over on his side. The water is nice and warm. Otto licks my face.

I soap him up and turn the hose on him. He shakes himself, spraying me with soapy water. I rinse him and he douses me again. He's giving me a bath, too.

After draining his tub, I take a towel from the dirty pile and dry him. He shakes himself out one more time and jumps out.

Otto circles in front of the oil furnace and lies down, perking his ears up and looking at me. I peel off my longjohns and socks and throw them in with my other dirty clothes in the water-filled tub. Mashing my stuff up and down a few times, I hang my rinsed clothes over the side of the tub. I pull the stopper out. The muddy water streams down to the floor drain.

I turn the hose on myself and soap up the washcloth my dad brought me. Otto's head rests on his paws. He watches me with one eye. He is the cleanest I ever saw him.

After rinsing myself, I dry off and put on clean clothes: a warm sweater, fresh longjohns—my pajamas in winter—and thick wool socks.

Otto is asleep. I'm not surprised. His day was as exciting as mine—and it's not over.

I go upstairs, leaving the door at the top of the steps open a crack for Otto to squeeze through when he wakes up. Mom is just putting supper on the table. I see a roast chicken and a bowl heaped with mashed potatoes. My mouth waters. She brings the gravy boat to the table.

"You look a darn sight better," Dad tells me.

"Come to the table," my mom says. "You're just in time."

"You left the basement door open again, Tony," my dad says, closing it.

"That's so Otto can come upstairs, Dad. He's sleeping in front of the furnace. I didn't want to wake him up."

My mom and dad look at each other and then at me. Dad carves the chicken.

Now that Otto is safely inside our house, my appetite has returned. I grab a chicken leg and thigh, and heap a mound of potatoes and corn onto my plate. Mom spoons salad onto the remaining space and Dad passes the gravy. I'd left a deep valley in my potato mountain for it.

"I know we can't give Otto chicken bones, Mom, but do we have anything else for him? It's Christmas Eve."

"I have some beef bones I was going to use to make soup. I can get more next week. There's not much meat on them, though," she tells me.

"Otto's not fussy," I remark. "He's very easy to get along with."

My mom and dad smile. I dive into my plate of food. For once, I don't have to sneak any of it from the table for Otto.

I help Mom clear the table and wash the dishes. Then I help Dad bring in some firewood. Maybe I don't need to butter them up any more, but it's Christmas Eve and I want to be nice to them. We go into the living room.

Dad turns on the lights on the tree. It's one of the best we've ever had. Mom turns off the lamps on the end tables. They take the sofa. I sit in one of the rockers in front of the hearth. The fire is blazing. I am warm and comfy—and very sleepy. I shut my eyes and rock.

———◦———

I am startled awake. There is scratching at the basement door. I jump to my feet and open it. Otto follows me into the living room. He sits at attention at the edge of the carpet. His shiny coat reflects the Christmas tree lights.

"Oh, my God," my mom says. "He's real. Otto's a real dog."

"Of course he is, Mom."

"He's a nice looking dog, Tony," my dad says. "And very well-behaved, it seems."

"Of course he is, Dad."

"Here, boy," my dad tells Otto.

Otto goes up to him, wagging his tail, and licks my dad's hand. Then he sits down at his feet.

Mom brings me the beef bone wrapped in brown butcher's paper. Otto's nose twitches. I put the bone down on the floor in front of the fireplace next to my rocking chair. Otto unwraps his Christmas bone with his paws and nudges aside the paper with his nose.

My mom goes back to the kitchen and returns with a tray of goodies: a plate of her Christmas cookies and three steaming glass mugs of apple cider. She's particular about who gets which mug, meaning she's poured some booze into hers and my dad's.

"Don't forget to leave a few cookies for Santa, you two," my mom warns me and my dad. "Otherwise he's not going to come."

"Santa Claus has already been here, Mom. I've got my Christmas wish. I've got Otto."

"I think you overlooked something else Santa left for you," my dad says, stooping over and retrieving a small package from beneath the tree. It is addressed to me. My hands shake as I unwrap and open it.

There is a card inside of a doggie in a wicker basket with a red ribbon tied around his neck. The card is signed "Santa." The dog looks an awful lot like Otto. He comes over to investigate the card and sniffs it.

In the small box, beneath where the card had been, is a red leather dog collar with a silver tag in the shape of a bone. Otto's name is engraved on it.

"Oh, my God. Mom. Dad. Santa Claus. Everybody," I shout.

Otto barks. He sits up and rests his paws on my knees. I put the red collar around his neck and buckle it. On the back of the silver dog tag is our address.

"Yelp woofbark, yip GROWL arf HOWL."

"That's right," I tell Otto, ruffling his fur.

My dog prances around the living room, showing off his new tag and collar. Mom pets his head; Dad scratches behind his ears.

I break an arm off one of the yellow sprinkled star cookies and offer it to him.

"No people food for Otto, Tony. That's rule Number One."

Otto continues gnawing his bone. I know he is happy. The crackling of the fire is comforting. I am happy, too.

After worrying his bone to death, Otto curls up at my feet. Between my faithful canine companion and my wool socks, my feet, which I thought would never thaw out, are warm and toasty. My head bobs to the rhythm of the rocker. I almost fall asleep again.

"Before you fall out of there and hurt yourself," my dad suggests, chuckling, "maybe you and Otto better get up to your room."

I climb up out of the rocker and Otto stirs. He looks up at me with the puppy eyes that first lured me to his cause. My dad ruffles my hair and hugs me; my mom gives me a kiss. We all wish one another a Merry Christmas, even Otto.

"YIP yap GROWL bark," he says.

Otto leads the way upstairs as though he knows where he's going, his doggie's tail slapping happily at my knees. By the time I get to my room and turn on the lamp, Otto is already curled up at the foot of my bed, right about where my feet will be.

About the Author

Brian Allan Skinner has written and published more than 120 short stories which appeared in small press and literary magazines, as well as anthologies, in the United States, Canada, and Ireland.

He is a former poetry and non-fiction reviewer for *Kirkus Reviews* and a production artist for *Scientific American Newsletters* in New York City. His two most recent collections of illustrated short fiction are "Shoot Me, Jesus: Tales of the Old & New Southwest" and "The Magic of Kindness: A Novel in Short Stories."

In 2015, Brian moved to Taos, New Mexico, which he first visited with his grandmother on a cross-country train trip aboard the Santa Fe Chief in 1960. He quickly settled into the thriving artistic and literary communities of Taos where he draws sustenance and inspiration from his many artist and writer friends.

The author, Christmas 1954, age five